THE TOYS OF PEACE
AND OTHER STORIES

ALSO BY SAKI

The Chronicles of Clovis
The Happy Cat: Beasts, Super-Beasts, and Monsters
Reginald
Reginald in Russia and Other Sketches

THE TOYS OF PEACE AND OTHER STORIES

SAKI

WILDSIDE PRESS: MMIII

THE TOYS OF PEACE

Published by:

Wildside Press
P.O. Box 301
Holicong, PA 18928-0301 U.S.A.
www.wildsidepress.com

Visit our web site for a list of new and classic books.

CONTENTS

THE TOYS OF PEACE

"Harvey," said Eleanor Bope, handing her brother a cutting from a London morning paper of the 19th of March, "just read this about children's toys, please; it exactly carries out some of our ideas about influence and upbringing."

"In the view of the National Peace Council," ran the extract, "there are grave objections to presenting our boys with regiments of fighting men, batteries of guns, and squadrons of 'Dreadnoughts.' Boys, the Council admits, naturally love fighting and all the panoply of war . . . but that is no reason for encouraging, and perhaps giving permanent form to, their primitive instincts. At the Children's Welfare Exhibition, which opens at Olympia in three weeks' time, the Peace Council will make an alternative suggestion to parents in the shape of an exhibition of 'peace toys.' In front of a specially-painted representation of the Peace Palace at The Hague will be grouped, not miniature soldiers but miniature civilians, not guns but ploughs and the tools of industry . . . It is hoped that manufacturers may take a hint from the exhibit, which will bear fruit in the toy shops."

"The idea is certainly an interesting and very well-meaning one," said Harvey; "whether it would succeed well in practice—"

"We must try," interrupted his sister; "you are coming down to us at Easter, and you always bring the boys some toys, so that will be an excellent opportunity for you to inaugurate the new experiment. Go about in the shops and buy any little toys and models that have special bearing on civilian life in its more peaceful aspects. Of course you must explain the toys to the children and interest them in the new idea. I regret to say that the 'Siege of Adrianople' toy, that their Aunt Susan sent them, didn't need any explanation; they knew all the uniforms and flags, and even the names of the respective commanders, and when I heard them one day using what seemed to be the most objectionable language they said it was Bulgarian words of command; of course it *may* have been, but at any rate I took the toy away from them. Now I shall expect your Easter gifts to give quite a new impulse and direction to the children's minds; Eric is not eleven yet, and Bertie is only nine-and-a-half, so they are really at a most impressionable age."

"There is primitive instinct to be taken into consideration, you know," said Henry doubtfully, "and hereditary tendencies as well. One of their great-uncles fought in the most intolerant fashion at Inkerman—he was specially mentioned in dispatches, I believe—and their great-grandfather smashed all his Whig neighbours' hot houses when the great Reform Bill was passed. Still, as you say, they are at an impressionable age. I will do my best."

On Easter Saturday Harvey Bope unpacked a large, promising-looking red cardboard box under the expectant eyes of his nephews. "Your uncle has brought you the newest thing in toys," Eleanor had said impressively, and youthful anticipation had been anxiously divided between Albanian soldiery and a Somali camel-corps. Eric was hotly in favour of the latter contingency. "There would be Arabs on horseback," he whispered; "the Albanians have got jolly uniforms, and they fight all day long, and all night, too, when there's a moon, but the country's rocky, so they've got no cavalry."

A quantity of crinkly paper shavings was the first thing that met the view when the lid was removed; the most exiting toys always began like that. Harvey pushed back the top layer and drew forth a square, rather featureless building.

"It's a fort!" exclaimed Bertie.

"It isn't, it's the palace of the Mpret of Albania," said Eric, immensely proud of his knowledge of the exotic title; "it's got no windows, you see, so that passers-by can't fire in at the Royal Family."

"It's a municipal dustbin," said Harvey hurriedly; "you see all the refuse and litter of a town is collected there, instead of lying about and injuring the health of the citizens."

In an awful silence he disinterred a little lead figure of a man in black clothes.

"That," he said, "is a distinguished civilian, John Stuart Mill. He was an authority on political economy."

"Why?" asked Bertie.

"Well, he wanted to be; he thought it was a useful thing to be."

Bertie gave an expressive grunt, which conveyed his opinion that there was no accounting for tastes.

Another square building came out, this time with windows and chimneys.

"A model of the Manchester branch of the Young Women's Christian Association," said Harvey.

"Are there any lions?" asked Eric hopefully. He had been reading Roman history and thought that where you found Christians you might reasonably expect to find a few lions.

"There are no lions," said Harvey. "Here is another civilian, Robert Raikes, the founder of Sunday schools, and here is a model of a municipal wash-house. These little round things are loaves backed in a sanitary bakehouse. That lead figure is a sanitary inspector, this one is a district councillor, and this one is an official of the Local Government Board."

"What does he do?" asked Eric wearily.

"He sees to things connected with his Department," said Harvey. "This box with a slit in it is a ballot-box. Votes are put into it at election times."

"What is put into it at other times?" asked Bertie.

"Nothing. And here are some tools of industry, a wheelbarrow and a hoe, and I think these are meant for hop poles. This is a model beehive, and that is a ventilator, for ventilating sewers. This seems to be another municipal dustbin—no, it is a model of a school of art and public library. This little lead figure is Mrs. Hemans, a poetess, and this is Rowland Hill, who introduced the system of penny postage. This is Sir John Herschel, the eminent astrologer."

"Are we to play with these civilian figures?" asked Eric.

"Of course," said Harvey, "these are toys; they are meant to be played with."

"But how?"

It was rather a poser. "You might make two of them contest a seat in Parliament," said Harvey, "and have an election—"

"With rotten eggs, and free fights, and ever so many broken heads!" exclaimed Eric.

"And noses all bleeding and everybody drunk as can be," echoed Bertie, who had carefully studied one of Hogarth's pictures.

"Nothing of the kind," said Harvey, "nothing in the least like that. Votes will be put in the ballot-box, and the Mayor will count them— and he will say which has received the most votes, and then the two candidates will thank him for presiding, and each will say that the contest has been conducted throughout in the pleasantest and most straightforward fashion, and they part with expressions of mutual esteem. There's a jolly game for you boys to play. I never had such toys when I was young."

"I don't think we'll play with them just now," said Eric, with an entire absence of the enthusiasm that his uncle had shown; "I think perhaps we ought to do a little of our holiday task. It's history this time; we've got to learn up something about the Bourbon period in France."

"The Bourbon period," said Harvey, with some disapproval in his voice.

"We've got to know something about Louis the Fourteenth," continued Eric; "I've learnt the names of all the principal battles already."

This would never do. "There were, of course, some battles fought during his reign," said Harvey, "but I fancy the accounts of them were much exaggerated; news was very unreliable in those days, and there were practically no war correspondents, so generals and commanders could magnify every little skirmish they engaged in till they reached the proportions of decisive battles. Louis was really famous, now, as a landscape gardener; the way he laid out Versailles was so much admired that it was copied all over Europe."

"Do you know anything about Madame Du Barry?" asked Eric; "didn't she have her head chopped off?"

"She was another great lover of gardening," said Harvey, evasively; "in fact, I believe the well known rose Du Barry was named after her, and now I think you had better play for a little and leave your lessons till later."

Harvey retreated to the library and spent some thirty or forty minutes in wondering whether it would be possible to compile a history, for use in elementary schools, in which there should be no prominent mention of battles, massacres, murderous intrigues, and violent deaths. The York and Lancaster period and the Napoleonic era would, he admitted to himself, present considerable difficulties, and the Thirty Years' War would entail something of a gap if you left it out altogether. Still, it would be something gained if, at a highly impressionable age, children could be got to fix their attention on the invention of calico printing instead of the Spanish Armada or the Battle of Waterloo.

It was time, he thought, to go back to the boys' room, and see how they were getting on with their peace toys. As he stood outside the door he could hear Eric's voice raised in command; Bertie chimed in now and again with a helpful suggestion.

"That is Louis the Fourteenth," Eric was saying, "that one in knee-breeches, that Uncle said invented Sunday schools. It isn't a bit like him, but it'll have to do."

"We'll give him a purple coat from my paintbox by and by," said Bertie.

"Yes, an' red heels. That is Madame de Maintenon, that one he called Mrs. Hemans. She begs Louis not to go on this expedition, but he turns a deaf ear. He takes Marshal Saxe with him, and we must pretend that they have thousands of men with them. The watchword is *Qui vive?* and the answer is *L'etat c'est moi*—that was one of his favourite remarks, you know. They land at Manchester in the dead of the night, and a Jacobite conspirator gives them the keys of the fortress."

Peeping in through the doorway Harvey observed that the municipal dustbin had been pierced with holes to accommodate the muzzles of imaginary cannon, and now represented the principal fortified position in Manchester; John Stuart Mill had been dipped in red ink, and apparently stood for Marshal Saxe.

"Louis orders his troops to surround the Young Women's Christian Association and seize the lot of them. 'Once back at the Louvre and the girls are mine,' he exclaims. We must use Mrs. Hemans again for one of the girls; she says 'Never,' and stabs Marshal Saxe to the heart."

"He bleeds dreadfully," exclaimed Bertie, splashing red ink liberally over the facade of the Association building.

"The soldiers rush in and avenge his death with the utmost savagery. A hundred girls are killed"—here Bertie emptied the remainder of the red ink over the devoted building—"and the surviving five hundred are dragged off to the French ships. 'I have lost a Marshal,' says Louis, 'but I do not go back empty-handed.'"

Harvey stole away from the room and sought out his sister.

"Eleanor," he said, "the experiment—"

"Yes?"

"Has failed. We have begun too late."

LOUISE

"THE TEA WILL be quite cold, you'd better ring for some more," said the Dowager Lady Beanford.

Susan Lady Beanford was a vigorous old woman who had coquetted with imaginary ill-health for the greater part of a lifetime; Clovis Sangrail irreverently declared that she had caught a chill at the Coronation of Queen Victoria and had never let it go again. Her sister, Jane Thropplestance, who was some years her junior, was chiefly remarkable for being the most absent-minded woman in Middlesex.

"I've really been unusually clever this afternoon," she remarked gaily, as she rang for the tea. "I've called on all the people I meant to call on; and I've done all the shopping that I set out to do. I even remembered to try and match that silk for you at Harrod's, but I'd forgotten to bring the pattern with me, so it was no use. I really think that was the only important thing I forgot during the whole afternoon. Quite wonderful for me, isn't it?"

"What have you done with Louise?" asked her sister. "Didn't you take her out with you? You said you were going to."

"Good gracious," exclaimed Jane, "what have I done with Louise? I must have left her somewhere."

"But where?"

"That's just it. Where have I left her? I can't remember if the Carrywoods were at home or if I just left cards. If there were at home I may have left Louise there to play bridge. I'll go and telephone to Lord Carrywood and find out."

"Is that you, Lord Carrywood?" she queried over the telephone; "it's me, Jane Thropplestance. I want to know, have you seen Louise?"

" 'Louise,' " came the answer, "it's been my fate to see it three times. At first, I must admit, I wasn't impressed by it, but the music grows on one after a bit. Still, I don't think I want to see it again just at present. Were you going to offer me a seat in your box?"

"Not the opera Louise—my niece, Louise Thropplestance. I

thought I might have left her at your house."

"You left cards on us this afternoon, I understand, but I don't think you left a niece. The footman would have been sure to have mentioned it if you had. Is it going to be a fashion to leave nieces on people as well as cards? I hope not; some of these houses in Berkeley-square have practically no accommodation for that sort of thing."

"She's not at the Carrywoods'," announced Jane, returning to her tea; "now I come to think of it, perhaps I left her at the silk counter at Selfridge's. I may have told her to wait there a moment while I went to look at the silks in a better light, and I may easily have forgotten about her when I found I hadn't your pattern with me. In that case she's still sitting there. She wouldn't move unless she was told to; Louise has no initiative."

"You said you tried to match the silk at Harrod's," interjected the dowager.

"Did I? Perhaps it was Harrod's. I really don't remember. It was one of those places where every one is so kind and sympathetic and devoted that one almost hates to take even a reel of cotton away from such pleasant surroundings."

"I think you might have taken Louise away. I don't like the idea of her being there among a lot of strangers. Supposing some unprincipled person was to get into conversation with her."

"Impossible. Louise has no conversation. I've never discovered a single topic on which she'd anything to say beyond 'Do you think so? I dare say you're right.' I really thought her reticence about the fall of the Ribot Ministry was ridiculous, considering how much her dear mother used to visit Paris. This bread and butter is cut far too thin; it crumbles away long before you can get it to your mouth. One feels so absurd, snapping at one's food in mid-air, like a trout leaping at may-fly."

"I am rather surprised," said the dowager, "that you can sit there making a hearty tea when you've just lost a favourite niece."

"You talk as if I'd lost her in a churchyard sense, instead of having temporarily mislaid her. I'm sure to remember presently where I left her."

"You didn't visit any place of devotion, did you? If you've left her mooning about Westminster Abbey or St. Peter's, Eaton Square, without being able to give any satisfactory reason why she's there, she'll be seized under the Cat and Mouse Act and sent to Reginald McKenna."

"That would be extremely awkward," said Jane, meeting an irresolute piece of bread and butter halfway; "we hardly know the McKennas, and it would be very tiresome having to telephone to some unsympathetic private secretary, describing Louise to him and asking to have her sent back in time for dinner. Fortunately, I didn't go to any place of devotion, though I did get mixed up with a Salvation Army procession. It was quite interesting to be at close quarters with them, they're so absolutely different to what they used to be when I first remember them in the 'eighties. They used to go about then unkempt and dishevelled, in a sort of smiling rage with the world, and now they're spruce and jaunty and flamboyantly decorative, like a geranium bed with religious convictions. Laura Kettleway was going on about them in the lift of the Dover Street Tube the other day, saying what a lot of good work they did, and what a loss it would have been if they'd never existed. 'If they had never existed,' I said, 'Granville Barker would have been certain to have invented something that looked exactly like them.' If you say things like that, quite loud, in a Tube lift, they always sound like epigrams."

"I think you ought to do something about Louise," said the dowager.

"I'm trying to think whether she was with me when I called on Ada Spelvexit. I rather enjoyed myself there. Ada was trying, as usual, to ram that odious Koriatoffski woman down my throat, knowing perfectly well that I detest her, and in an unguarded moment she said: 'She's leaving her present house and going to Lower Seymour Street.' 'I dare say she will, if she stays there long enough,' I said. Ada didn't see it for about three minutes, and then she was positively uncivil. No, I am certain I didn't leave Louise there."

"If you could manage to remember where you *did* leave her, it would be more to the point than these negative assurances," said Lady Beanford; "so far, all we know is that she is not at the Carrywoods', or

Ada Spelvexit's, or Westminster Abbey."

"That narrows the search down a bit," said Jane hopefully; "I rather fancy she must have been with me when I went to Mornay's. I know I went to Mornay's, because I remember meeting that delightful Malcolm What's-his-name there—you know whom I mean. That's the great advantage of people having unusual first names, you needn't try and remember what their other name is. Of course I know one or two other Malcolms, but none that could possibly be described as delightful. He gave me two tickets for the Happy Sunday Evenings in Sloane Square. I've probably left them at Mornay's, but still it was awfully kind of him to give them to me."

"Do you think you left Louise there?"

"I might telephone and ask. Oh, Robert, before you clear the tea-things away I wish you'd ring up Mornay's, in Regent Street, and ask if I left two theatre tickets and one niece in their shop this afternoon."

"A niece, ma'am?" asked the footman.

"Yes, Miss Louise didn't come home with me, and I'm not sure where I left her."

"Miss Louise has been upstairs all the afternoon, ma'am, reading to the second kitchenmaid, who has the neuralgia. I took up tea to Miss Louise at a quarter to five o'clock, ma'am."

"Of course, how silly of me. I remember now, I asked her to read the Faerie Queene to poor Emma, to try to send her to sleep. I always get some one to read the Faerie Queene to me when I have neuralgia, and it usually sends me to sleep. Louise doesn't seem to have been successful, but one can't say she hasn't tried. I expect after the first hour or so the kitchenmaid would rather have been left alone with her neuralgia, but of course Louise wouldn't leave off till some one told her to. Anyhow, you can ring up Mornay's, Robert, and ask whether I left two theatre tickets there. Except for your silk, Susan, those seem to be the only things I've forgotten this afternoon. Quite wonderful for me."

TEA

JAMES CUSHAT-PRINKLY was a young man who had always had a settled conviction that one of these days he would marry; up to the age of thirty-four he had done nothing to justify that conviction. He liked and admired a great many women collectively and dispassionately without singling out one for especial matrimonial consideration, just as one might admire the Alps without feeling that one wanted any particular peak as one's own private property. His lack of initiative in this matter aroused a certain amount of impatience among the sentimentally-minded women-folk of his home circle; his mother, his sisters, an aunt-in-residence, and two or three intimate matronly friends regarded his dilatory approach to the married state with a disapproval that was far from being inarticulate. His most innocent flirtations were watched with the straining eagerness which a group of unexercised terriers concentrates on the slightest movements of a human being who may be reasonably considered likely to take them for a walk. No decent-souled mortal can long resist the pleading of several pairs of walk-beseeching dog-eyes; James Cushat-Prinkly was not sufficiently obstinate or indifferent to home influences to disregard the obviously expressed wish of his family that he should become enamoured of some nice marriageable girl, and when his Uncle Jules departed this life and bequeathed him a comfortable little legacy it really seemed the correct thing to do to set about discovering some one to share it with him. The process of discovery was carried on more by the force of suggestion and the weight of public opinion than by any initiative of his own; a clear working majority of his female relatives and the aforesaid matronly friends had pitched on Joan Sebastable as the most suitable young woman in his range of acquaintance to whom he might propose marriage, and James became gradually accustomed to the idea that he and Joan would go together through the prescribed stages of congratulations, present-receiving, Norwegian or Mediterranean hotels, and eventual domesticity. It was necessary, however to ask the lady what she thought about the matter; the family had so far con-

ducted and directed the flirtation with ability and discretion, but the actual proposal would have to be an individual effort.

Cushat-Prinkly walked across the Park towards the Sebastable residence in a frame of mind that was moderately complacent. As the thing
was going to be done he was glad to feel that he was going to get it settled
and off his mind that afternoon. Proposing marriage, even to a nice girl
like Joan, was a rather irksome business, but one could not have a honeymoon in Minorca and a subsequent life of married happiness without
such preliminary. He wondered what Minorca was really like as a place
to stop in; in his mind's eye it was an island in perpetual half-mourning,
with black or white Minorca hens running all over it. Probably it would
not be a bit like that when one came to examine it. People who had been
in Russia had told him that they did not remember having seen any
Muscovy ducks there, so it was possible that there would be no Minorca
fowls on the island.

His Mediterranean musings were interrupted by the sound of a
clock striking the half-hour. Half-past four. A frown of dissatisfaction
settled on his face. He would arrive at the Sebastable mansion just at the
hour of afternoon tea. Joan would be seated at a low table, spread with an
array of silver kettles and cream-jugs and delicate porcelain teacups, behind which her voice would tinkle pleasantly in a series of little friendly
questions about weak or strong tea, how much, if any, sugar, milk,
cream, and so forth. "Is it one lump? I forgot. You do take milk, don't
you? Would you like some more hot water, if it's too strong?"

Cushat-Prinkly had read of such things in scores of novels, and hundreds of actual experiences had told him that they were true to life.
Thousands of women, at this solemn afternoon hour, were sitting behind dainty porcelain and silver fittings, with their voices tinkling pleasantly in a cascade of solicitous little questions. Cushat-Prinkly detested
the whole system of afternoon tea. According to his theory of life a
woman should lie on a divan or couch, talking with incomparable
charm or looking unutterable thoughts, or merely silent as a thing to be
looked on, and from behind a silken curtain a small Nubian page should
silently bring in a tray with cups and dainties, to be accepted silently, as a

matter of course, without drawn-out chatter about cream and sugar and hot water. If one's soul was really enslaved at one's mistress's feet how could one talk coherently about weakened tea? Cushat-Prinkly had never expounded his views on the subject to his mother; all her life she had been accustomed to tinkle pleasantly at tea-time behind dainty porcelain and silver, and if he had spoken to her about divans and Nubian pages she would have urged him to take a week's holiday at the seaside. Now, as he passed through a tangle of small streets that led indirectly to the elegant Mayfair terrace for which he was bound, a horror at the idea of confronting Joan Sebastable at her tea-table seized on him. A momentary deliverance presented itself; on one floor of a narrow little house at the noisier end of Esquimault Street lived Rhoda Ellam, a sort of remote cousin, who made a living by creating hats out of costly materials. The hats really looked as if they had come from Paris; the cheques she got for them unfortunately never looked as if they were going to Paris. However, Rhoda appeared to find life amusing and to have a fairly good time in spite of her straitened circumstances. Cushat-Prinkly decided to climb up to her floor and defer by half an hour or so the important business which lay before him; by spinning out his visit he could contrive to reach the Sebastable mansion after the last vestiges of dainty porcelain had been cleared away.

Rhoda welcomed him into a room that seemed to do duty as workshop, sitting-room, and kitchen combined, and to be wonderfully clean and comfortable at the same time.

"I'm having a picnic meal," she announced. "There's caviare in that jar at your elbow. Begin on that brown bread-and-butter while I cut some more. Find yourself a cup; the teapot is behind you. Now tell me about hundreds of things."

She made no other allusion to food, but talked amusingly and made her visitor talk amusingly too. At the same time she cut the bread-and-butter with a masterly skill and produced red pepper and sliced lemon, where so many women would merely have produced reasons and regrets for not having any. Cushat-Prinkly found that he was enjoying an excellent tea without having to answer as many questions about it as a Minister for Agriculture might be called on to reply to during an outbreak of cattle plague.

"And now tell me why you have come to see me," said Rhoda suddenly. "You arouse not merely my curiosity but my business instincts. I hope you've come about hats. I heard that you had come into a legacy the other day, and, of course, it struck me that it would be a beautiful and desirable thing for you to celebrate the event by buying brilliantly expensive hats for all your sisters. They may not have said anything about it, but I feel sure the same idea has occurred to them. Of course, with Goodwood on us, I am rather rushed just now, but in my business we're accustomed to that; we live in a series of rushes—like the infant Moses."

"I didn't come about hats," said her visitor. "In fact, I don't think I really came about anything. I was passing and I just thought I'd look in and see you. Since I've been sitting talking to you, however, rather important idea has occurred to me. If you'll forget Goodwood for a moment and listen to me, I'll tell you what it is."

Some forty minutes later James Cushat-Prinkly returned to the bosom of his family, bearing an important piece of news.

"I'm engaged to be married," he announced.

A rapturous outbreak of congratulation and self-applause broke out.

"Ah, we knew! We saw it coming! We foretold it weeks ago!"

"I'll bet you didn't," said Cushat-Prinkly. "If any one had told me at lunch-time today that I was going to ask Rhoda Ellam to marry me and that she was going to accept me I would have laughed at the idea."

The romantic suddenness of the affair in some measure compensated James's women-folk for the ruthless negation of all their patient effort and skilled diplomacy. It was rather trying to have to deflect their enthusiasm at a moment's notice from Joan Sebastable to Rhoda Ellam; but, after all, it was James's wife who was in question, and his tastes had some claim to be considered.

On a September afternoon of the same year, after the honeymoon in Minorca had ended, Cushat-Prinkly came into the drawing-room of

his new house in Granchester Square. Rhoda was seated at a low table, behind a service of dainty porcelain and gleaming silver. There was a pleasant tinkling note in her voice as she handed him a cup.

"You like it weaker than that, don't you? Shall I put some more hot
water to it? No?"

THE DISAPEARANCE OF CRISPINA UMBERLEIGH

IN A FIRST-CLASS carriage of a train speeding Balkanward across the flat, green Hungarian plain two Britons sat in friendly, fitful converse. They had first foregathered in the cold grey dawn at the frontier line, where the presiding eagle takes on an extra head and Teuton lands pass from Hohenzollern to Habsburg keeping—and where a probing official beak requires to delve in polite and perhaps perfunctory, but always tiresome, manner into the baggage of sleep-hungry passengers. After a day's break of their journey at Vienna the travellers had again foregathered at the trainside and paid one another the compliment of settling instinctively into the same carriage. The elder of the two had the appearance and manner of a diplomat; in point of fact he was the well-connected foster-brother of a wine business. The other was certainly a journalist. Neither man was talkative and each was grateful to the other for not being talkative. That is why from time to time they talked.

One topic of conversation naturally thrust itself forward in front of all others. In Vienna the previous day they had learned of the mysterious vanishing of a world-famous picture from the walls of the Louvre.

"A dramatic disappearance of that sort is sure to produce a crop of imitations," said the Journalist.

"It has had a lot of anticipations, for the matter of that," said the Wine-brother.

"Oh, of course there have been thefts from the Louvre before."

"I was thinking of the spiriting away of human beings rather than pictures. In particular I was thinking of the case of my aunt, Crispina Umberleigh."

"I remember hearing something of the affair," said the Journalist, "but I was away from England at the time. I never quite knew what was supposed to have happened."

"You may hear what really happened if you will respect it as a confidence," said the Wine Merchant. "In the first place I may say that the disappearance of Mrs. Umberleigh was not regarded by the family entirely as a bereavement. My uncle, Edward Umberleigh, was not by any means a weak-kneed individual, in fact in the world of politics he had to be reckoned with more or less as a strong man, but he was unmistakably dominated by Crispina; indeed I never met any human being who was not frozen into subjection when brought into prolonged contact with her. Some people are born to command; Crispina Mrs. Umberleigh was born to legislate, codify, administrate, censor, license, ban, execute, and sit in judgement generally. If she was not born with that destiny she adopted it at an early age. From the kitchen regions upwards every one in the household came under her despotic sway and stayed there with the submissiveness of molluscs involved in a glacial epoch. As a nephew on a footing of only occasional visits she affected me merely as an epidemic, disagreeable while it lasted, but without any permanent effect; but her own sons and daughters stood in mortal awe of her; their studies, friendships, diet, amusements, religious observances, and way of doing their hair were all regulated and ordained according to the august lady's will and pleasure. This will help you to understand the sensation of stupefaction which was caused in the family when she unobtrusively and inexplicably vanished. It was as though St. Paul's Cathedral or the Piccadilly Hotel had disappeared in the night, leaving nothing but an open space to mark where it had stood. As far as was known nothing was troubling her; in fact there was much before her to make life particularly well worth living. The youngest boy had come back from school with an unsatisfactory report, and she was to have sat in judgement on him the very afternoon of the day she disappeared—if it had been he who had vanished in a hurry one could have supplied the motive. Then she was in the middle of a newspaper correspondence with a rural dean in which she had already proved him guilty of heresy, inconsistency, and unworthy quibbling, and no ordinary consideration would have induced her to discontinue the controversy. Of course the matter was put in the hands of the police, but as far as possible it was kept out of the papers, and the generally accepted explanation of her withdrawal from her social circle was that she had gone into a nursing home."

"And what was the immediate effect on the home circle?" asked the Journalist.

"All the girls bought themselves bicycles; the feminine cycling craze was still in existence, and Crispina had rigidly vetoed any participation in it among the members of her household. The youngest boy let himself go to such an extent during his next term that it had to be his last as far as that particular establishment was concerned. The elder boys propounded a theory that their mother might be wandering somewhere abroad, and searched for her assiduously, chiefly, it must be admitted, in a class of Montmartre resort where it was extremely improbable that she would be found."

"And all this while couldn't your uncle get hold of the least clue?"

"As a matter of fact he had received some information, though of course I did not know of it at the time. He got a message one day telling him that his wife had been kidnapped and smuggled out of the country; she was said to be hidden away, in one of the islands off the coast of Norway I think it was, in comfortable surroundings and well cared for. And with the information came a demand for money; a lump sum of 2000 pounds was to be paid yearly. Failing this she would be immediately restored to her family."

The Journalist was silent for a moment, and them began to laugh quietly.

"It was certainly an inverted form of holding to ransom," he said.

"If you had known my aunt," said the Wine Merchant, "you would have wondered that they didn't put the figure higher."

"I realise the temptation. Did your uncle succumb to it?"

"Well, you see, he had to think of others as well as himself. For the family to have gone back into the Crispina thraldom after having tasted the delights of liberty would have been a tragedy, and there were even wider considerations to be taken into account. Since his bereavement he had unconsciously taken up a far bolder and more initiatory line in public affairs, and his popularity and influence had increased correspondingly. From being merely a strong man in the political world he began to be spoken of as the strong man. All this he knew would be jeopardised if he once more dropped into the social position of the husband of Mrs. Umberleigh. He was a rich man, and the 2000 pounds a year, though not exactly a fleabite, did not seem an extravagant price to pay for the boarding-out of Crispina. Of course, he had severe qualms of conscience about the arrangement. Later on, when he took me into his confidence, he told me that in paying the ransom, or hush-money as I should have called it, he was partly influenced by the fear that if he refused it the kidnappers might have vented their rage and disappointment on their captive. It was better, he said, to think of her being well cared for as a highly-valued paying guest in one of the Lofoden Islands than to have her struggling miserably home in a maimed and mutilated condition. Anyway he paid the yearly instalment as punctually as one pays a fire insurance, and with equal promptitude there would come an acknowledgment of the money and a brief statement to the effect that Crispina was in good health and fairly cheerful spirits. One report even mentioned that she was busying herself with a scheme for proposed reforms in Church management to be pressed on the local pastorate. Another spoke of a rheumatic attack and a journey to a 'cure' on the mainland, and on that occasion an additional eighty pounds was demanded and conceded. Of course it was to the interest of the kidnappers to keep their charge in good health, but the secrecy with which they managed to shroud their arrangements argued a really wonderful organisation. If my uncle was paying a rather high price, at least he could console himself with the reflection that he was paying specialists' fees."

"Meanwhile had the police given up all attempts to track the missing lady?" asked the Journalist.

"Not entirely; they came to my uncle from time to time to report on clues which they thought might yield some elucidation as to her fate or whereabouts, but I think they had their suspicions that he was possessed of more information than he had put at their disposal. And then, after a disappearance of more than eight years, Crispina returned with dramatic suddenness to the home she had left so mysteriously."

"She had given her captors the slip?"

"She had never been captured. Her wandering away had been caused by a sudden and complete loss of memory. She usually dressed rather in the style of a superior kind of charwoman, and it was not so very surprising that she should have imagined that she was one; and still less that people should accept her statement and help her to get work. She had wandered as far afield as Birmingham, and found fairly steady employment there, her energy and enthusiasm in putting people's rooms in order counterbalancing her obstinate and domineering characteristics. It was the shock of being patronisingly addressed as 'my good woman' by a curate, who was disputing with her where the stove should be placed in a parish concert hall that led to the sudden restoration of her memory. 'I think you forget who you are speaking to,' she observed crushingly, which was rather unduly severe, considering she had only just remembered it herself."

"But," exclaimed the Journalist, "the Lofoden Island people! Who had they got hold of?"

"A purely mythical prisoner. It was an attempt in the first place by some one who knew something of the domestic situation, probably a discharged valet, to bluff a lump sum out of Edward Umberleigh before the missing woman turned up; the subsequent yearly instalments were an unlooked-for increment to the original haul.

"Crispina found that the eight years' interregnum had materially weakened her ascendancy over her now grown-up offspring. Her husband, however, never accomplished anything great in the political world after her return; the strain of trying to account satisfactorily for an unspecified expenditure of sixteen thousand pounds spread over eight years sufficiently occupied his mental energies. Here is Belgrad and another custom house."

THE WOLVES OF CERNOGRATZ

"ARE THERE any old legends attached to the castle?" asked Conrad of his sister. Conrad was a prosperous Hamburg merchant, but he was the one poetically dispositioned member of an eminently practical family.

The Baroness Gruebel shrugged her plump shoulders.

"There are always legends hanging about these old places. They are not difficult to invent, and they cost nothing. In this case there is a story that when anyone dies in the castle, all the dogs in the village and the wild beasts in forest howl the night long. It would not be pleasant to listen to, would it?"

"It would be weird and romantic," said the Hamburg merchant.

"Anyhow, it isn't true," said the Baroness complacently. "Since we bought the place, we have had proof that nothing of the sort happens. When the old mother-in-law died last springtime, we all listened, but there was no howling. It is just a story that lends dignity to the place without costing anything."

"The story is not as you have told it," said Amalie, the grey old governess. Every one turned and looked at her in astonishment. She was wont to sit silent and prim and faded in her place at table, never speaking unless some one spoke to her, and there were few who troubled themselves to make conversation with her. Today a sudden volubility had descended on her; she continued to talk, rapidly and nervously, looking straight in front of her and seeming to address no one in particular.

"It is not when any one dies in the castle that the howling is heard. It was when one of the Cernogratz family died here that the wolves came from far and near and howled at the edge of the forest just before the death hour. There were only a few couple of wolves that had their lairs in this part of the forest, but at such a time the keepers say there would be scores of them, gliding about in the shadows and howling in chorus, and the dogs of the castle and the village and all the farms round would bay and howl in fear and anger at the wolf chorus, and as the soul of the dying one left its body a tree would crash down in the park. That is what happened when a Cernogratz died in his family castle. But for a stranger dying here, of course no wolf would howl and no tree would fall. Oh, no."

There was a note of defiance, almost of contempt, in her voice as she said the last words. The well-fed, much-too-well dressed Baroness stared angrily at the dowdy old woman who had come forth from her usual and seemly position of effacement to speak so disrespectfully.

"You seem to know quite a lot about the von Cernogratz legends, Fraulein Schmidt," she said sharply; "I did not know that family histories were among the subjects you are supposed to be proficient in."

The answer to her taunt was even more unexpected and astonishing than the conversational outbreak which had provoked it.

"I am a von Cernogratz myself," said the old woman, "that is why I know the family history."

"You a von Cernogratz? You!" came in an incredulous chorus.

"When we became very poor," she explained, "and I had to go out and give teaching lessons, I took another name; I thought it would be more in keeping. But my grandfather spent much of his time as a boy in this castle, and my father used to tell me many stories about it, and, of course, I knew all the family legends and stories. When one has nothing left to one but memories, one guards and dusts them with especial care. I little thought when I took service with you that I should one day come with you to the old home of my family. I could wish it had been anywhere else."

There was silence when she finished speaking, and then the Baroness turned the conversation to a less embarrassing topic than family histories. But afterwards, when the old governess had slipped away quietly to her duties, there arose a clamour of derision and disbelief.

"It was an impertinence," snapped out the Baron, his protruding eyes taking on a scandalised expression; "fancy the woman talking like that at our table. She almost told us we were nobodies, and I don't believe a word of it. She is just Schmidt and nothing more. She has been talking to some of the peasants about the old Cernogratz family, and raked up their history and their stories."

"She wants to make herself out of some consequence," said the Baroness; "she knows she will soon be past work and she wants to appeal to our sympathies. Her grandfather, indeed!"

The Baroness had the usual number of grandfathers, but she never, never boasted about them.

"I dare say her grandfather was a pantry boy or something of the sort in the castle," sniggered the Baron; "that part of the story may be true."

The merchant from Hamburg said nothing; he had seen tears in the old woman's eyes when she spoke of guarding her memories—or, being of an imaginative disposition, he thought he had.

"I shall give her notice to go as soon as the New Year festivities are over," said the Baroness; "till then I shall be too busy to manage without her."

But she had to manage without her all the same, for in the cold biting weather after Christmas, the old governess fell ill and kept to her room.

"It is most provoking," said the Baroness, as her guests sat round the fire on one of the last evenings of the dying year; "all the time that she has been with us I cannot remember that she was ever seriously ill, too ill to go about and do her work, I mean. And now, when I have the house full, and she could be useful in so many ways, she goes and breaks down. One is sorry for her, of course, she looks so withered and shrunken, but it is intensely annoying all the same."

"Most annoying," agreed the banker's wife, sympathetically; "it is the intense cold, I expect, it breaks the old people up. It has been unusually cold this year."

"The frost is the sharpest that has been known in December for many years," said the Baron.

"And, of course, she is quite old," said the Baroness; "I wish I had given her notice some weeks ago, then she would have left before this happened to her. Why, Wappi, what is the matter with you?"

The small, woolly lapdog had leapt suddenly down from its cushion and crept shivering under the sofa. At the same moment an outburst of angry barking came from the dogs in the castle yard, and other dogs could be heard yapping and barking in the distance.

"What is disturbing the animals?" asked the Baron.

And then the humans, listening intently, heard the sound that had roused the dogs to their demonstrations of fear and rage; heard a long-drawn whining howl, rising and falling, seeming at one moment leagues away, at others sweeping across the snow until it appeared to come from the foot of the castle walls. All the starved, cold misery of a frozen world, all the relentless hunger-fury of the wild, blended with other forlorn and haunting melodies to which one could give no name, seemed concentrated in that wailing cry.

"Wolves!" cried the Baron.

Their music broke forth in one raging burst, seeming to come from everywhere.

"Hundreds of wolves," said the Hamburg merchant, who was a man of strong imagination.

Moved by some impulse which she could not have explained, the Baroness left her guests and made her way to the narrow, cheerless room where the old governess lay watching the hours of the drying year slip by. In spite of the biting cold of the winter night, the window stood open. With a scandalised exclamation on her lips, the Baroness rushed forward to close it.

"Leave it open," said the old woman in a voice that for all its weakness carried an air of command such as the Baroness had never heard before from her lips.

"But you will die of cold!" she expostulated.

"I am dying in any case," said the voice, "and I want to hear their music. They have come from far and wide to sing the death-music of my family. It is beautiful that they have come; I am the last von Cernogratz that will die in our old castle, and they have come to sing to me. Hark, how loud they are calling!"

The cry of the wolves rose on the still winter air and floated round the castle walls in long-drawn piercing wails; the old woman lay back on her couch with a look of long-delayed happiness on her face.

"Go away," she said to the Baroness; "I am not lonely any more. I am one of a great old family . . . "

"I think she is dying," said the Baroness when she had rejoined her guests; "I suppose we must send for a doctor. And that terrible howling! Not for much money would I have such death-music."

"That music is not to be bought for any amount of money," said Conrad.

"Hark! What is that other sound?" asked the Baron, as a noise of splitting and crashing was heard.

It was a tree falling in the park.

There was a moment of constrained silence, and then the banker's wife spoke.

"It is the intense cold that is splitting the trees. It is also the cold that has brought the wolves out in such numbers. It is many years since we have had such a cold winter."

The Baroness eagerly agreed that the cold was responsible for these things. It was the cold of the open window, too, which caused the heart failure that made the doctor's ministrations unnecessary for the old Fraulein. But the notice in the newspapers looked very well—

"On December 29th, at Schloss Cernogratz, Amalie von Cerno-gratz, for many years the valued friend of Baron and Baroness Gruebel."

LOUIS

"IT WOULD be jolly to spend Easter in Vienna this year," said Strudwarden, "and look up some of my old friends there. It's about the jolliest place I know of to be at for Easter—"

"I thought we had made up our minds to spend Easter at Brighton," interrupted Lena Strudwarden, with an air of aggrieved surprise.

"You mean that you had made up your mind that we should spend Easter there," said her husband; "we spent last Easter there, and Whitsuntide as well, and the year before that we were at Worthing, and Brighton again before that. I think it would be just as well to have a real change of scene while we are about it."

"The journey to Vienna would be very expensive," said Lena.

"You are not often concerned about economy," said Strudwarden, "and in any case the trip of Vienna won't cost a bit more than the rather meaningless luncheon parties we usually give to quite meaningless acquaintances at Brighton. To escape from all that set would be a holiday in itself."

Strudwarden spoke feelingly; Lena Strudwarden maintained an equally feeling silence on that particular subject. The set that she gathered round her at Brighton and other South Coast resorts was composed of individuals who might be dull and meaningless in themselves, but who understood the art of flattering Mrs. Strudwarden. She had no intention of foregoing their society and their homage and flinging herself among unappreciative strangers in a foreign capital.

"You must go to Vienna alone if you are bent on going," she said; "I couldn't leave Louis behind, and a dog is always a fearful nuisance in a foreign hotel, besides all the fuss and separation of the quarantine restrictions when one comes back. Louis would die if he was parted from me for even a week. You don't know what that would mean to me."

Lena stooped down and kissed the nose of the diminutive brown Pomeranian that lay, snug and irresponsive, beneath a shawl on her lap.

"Look here," said Strudwarden, "this eternal Louis business is getting to be a ridiculous nuisance. Nothing can be done, no plans can be made, without some veto connected with that animal's whims or convenience being imposed. If you were a priest in attendance on some African fetish you couldn't set up a more elaborate code of restrictions. I believe you'd ask the Government to put off a General Election if you thought it would interfere with Louis's comfort in any way."

By way of answer to this tirade Mrs. Strudwarden stooped down again and kissed the irresponsive brown nose. It was the action of a woman with a beautifully meek nature, who would, however, send the whole world to the stake sooner than yield an inch where she knew herself to be in the right.

"It isn't as if you were in the least bit fond of animals," went on Strudwarden, with growing irritation; "when we are down at Kerryfield you won't stir a step to take the house dogs out, even if they're dying for a run, and I don't think you've been in the stables twice in your life. You laugh at what you call the fuss that's being made over the extermination of plumage birds, and you are quite indignant with me if I interfere on behalf of an ill-treated, over-driven animal on the road. And yet you insist on every one's plans being made subservient to the convenience of that stupid little morsel of fur and selfishness."

"You are prejudiced against my little Louis," said Lena, with a world of tender regret in her voice.

"I've never had the chance of being anything else but prejudiced against him," said Strudwarden; "I know what a jolly responsive companion a doggie can be, but I've never been allowed to put a finger near Louis. You say he snaps at any one except you and your maid, and you snatched him away from old Lady Peterby the other day, when she wanted to pet him, for fear he would bury his teeth in her. All that I ever see of him is the top of his unhealthy-looking little nose, peeping out from his basket or from your muff, and I occasionally hear his wheezy little bark when you take him for a walk up and down the corridor. You can't expect one to get extravagantly fond of a dog of that sort. One might as well work up an affection for the cuckoo in a cuckoo-clock."

"He loves me," said Lena, rising from the table, and bearing the shawl-swathed Louis in her arms. "He loves only me, and perhaps that is why I love him so much in return. I don't care what you say against him, I am not going to be separated from him. If you insist on going to Vienna you must go alone, as far as I am concerned. I think it would be much more sensible if you were to come to Brighton with Louis and me, but of course you must please yourself."

"You must get rid of that dog," said Strudwarden's sister when Lena had left the room; "it must be helped to some sudden and merciful end. Lena is merely making use of it as an instrument for getting her own way on dozens of occasions when she would otherwise be obliged to yield gracefully to your wishes or to the general convenience. I am convinced that she doesn't care a brass button about the animal itself. When her friends are buzzing round her at Brighton or anywhere else and the dog would be in the way, it has to spend whole days alone with the maid, but if you want Lena to go with you anywhere where she doesn't want to go instantly she trots out the excuse that she couldn't be separated from her dog. Have you ever come into a room unobserved and heard Lena talking to her beloved pet? I never have. I believe she only fusses over it when there's some one present to notice her."

"I don't mind admitting," said Strudwarden, "that I've dwelt more than once lately on the possibility of some fatal accident putting an end to Louis's existence. It's not very easy, though, to arrange a fatality for a creature that spends most of its time in a muff or asleep in a toy kennel. I don't think poison would be any good; it's obviously horribly over-fed, for I've seen Lena offer it dainties at table sometimes, but it never seems to eat them."

"Lena will be away at church on Wednesday morning," said Elsie Strudwarden reflectively; "she can't take Louis with her there, and she is going on to the Dellings for lunch. That will give you several hours in which to carry out your purpose. The maid will be flirting with the chauffeur most of the time, and, anyhow, I can manage to keep her out of the way on some pretext or other."

"That leaves the field clear," said Strudwarden, "but unfortunately my brain is equally a blank as far as any lethal project is concerned. The little beast is so monstrously inactive; I can't pretend that it leapt into the bath and drowned itself, or that it took on the butcher's mastiff in unequal combat and got chewed up. In what possible guise could death come to a confirmed basket-dweller? It would be too suspicious if we invented a Suffragette raid and pretended that they invaded Lena's boudoir and threw a brick at him. We should have to do a lot of other damage as well, which would be rather a nuisance, and the servants would think it odd that they had seen nothing of the invaders."

"I have an idea," said Elsie; "get a box with an airtight lid, and bore a small hole in it, just big enough to let in an indiarubber tube. Pop Louis, kennel and all, into the box, shut it down, and put the other end of the tube over the gas-bracket. There you have a perfect lethal chamber. You can stand the kennel at the open window afterwards, to get rid of the smell of gas, and all that Lena will find when she comes home late in the afternoon will be a placidly defunct Louis."

"Novels have been written about women like you," said Strudwarden; "you have a perfectly criminal mind. Let's come and look for a box."

Two mornings later the conspirators stood gazing guiltily at a stout square box, connected with the gas-bracket by a length of indiarubber tubing.

"Not a sound," said Elsie; "he never stirred; it must have been quite painless. All the same I feel rather horrid now it's done."

"The ghastly part has to come," said Strudwarden, turning off the gas. "We'll lift the lid slowly, and let the gas out by degrees. Swing the door to and fro to send a draught through the room."

Some minutes later, when the fumes had rushed off, he stooped down and lifted out the little kennel with its grim burden. Elsie gave an exclamation of terror. Louis sat at the door of his dwelling, head erect and ears pricked, as coldly and defiantly inert as when they had put him into his execution chamber. Strudwarden dropped the kennel with a jerk, and stared for a long moment at the miracle-dog; then he went into a peal of chattering laughter.

It was certainly a wonderful imitation of a truculent-looking toy

Pomeranian, and the apparatus that gave forth a wheezy bark when you pressed it had materially helped the imposition that Lena, and Lena's maid, had foisted on the household. For a woman who disliked animals, but liked getting her own way under a halo of unselfishness, Mrs. Strudwarden had managed rather well.

"Louis is dead," was the curt information that greeted Lena on her return from her luncheon party.

"Louis *dead!*" she exclaimed.

"Yes, he flew at the butcher-boy and bit him, and he bit me, too, when I tried to get him off, so I had to have him destroyed. You warned me that he snapped, but you didn't tell me that he was downright dangerous. I shall have to pay the boy something heavy by way of compensation, so you will have to go without those buckles that you wanted to have for Easter; also I shall have to go to Vienna to consult Dr. Schroeder, who is a specialist on dog-bites, and you will have to come too. I have sent what remains of Louis to Rowland Ward to be stuffed; that will be my Easter gift to you instead of the buckles. For Heaven's sake, Lena, weep, if you really feel it so much; anything would be better than standing there staring as if you thought I had lost my reason."

Lena Strudwarden did not weep, but her attempt at laughing was an unmistakable failure.

THE GUESTS

"THE LANDSCAPE seen from our windows is certainly charming," said Annabel; "those cherry orchards and green meadows, and the river winding along the valley, and the church tower peeping out among the elms, they all make a most effective picture. There's something dreadfully sleepy and languorous about it, though; stagnation seems to be the dominant note. Nothing ever happens here; seedtime and harvest, an occasional outbreak of measles or a mildly destructive thunderstorm, and a little election excitement about once in five years, that is all that we have to modify the monotony of our existence. Rather dreadful, isn't it?"

"On the contrary," said Matilda, "I find it soothing and restful; but then, you see, I've lived in countries where things do happen, ever so many at a time, when you're not ready for them happening all at once."

"That, of course, makes a difference," said Annabel.

"I have never forgotten," said Matilda, "the occasion when the Bishop of Bequar paid us an unexpected visit; he was on his way to lay the foundation-stone of a mission-house or something of the sort."

"I thought that out there you were always prepared for emergency guests turning up," said Annabel.

"I was quite prepared for half a dozen Bishops," said Matilda, "but it was rather disconcerting to find out after a little conversation that this particular one was a distant cousin of mine, belonging to a branch of the family that had quarrelled bitterly and offensively with our branch about a Crown Derby dessert service; they got it, and we ought to have got it, in some legacy, or else we got it and they thought they ought to have it, I forget which; anyhow, I know they behaved disgracefully. Now here was one of them turning up in the odour of sanctity, so to speak, and claiming the traditional hospitality of the East."

"It was rather trying, but you could have left your husband to do most of the entertaining."

"My husband was fifty miles upcountry, talking sense, or what he imagined to be sense, to a village community that fancied one of their leading men was a weretiger."

"A what tiger?"

"A weretiger; you've heard of werewolves, haven't you, a mixture of wolf and human being and demon? Well, in those parts they have weretigers, or think they have, and I must say that in this case, so far as sworn and uncontested evidence went, they had every ground for thinking so. However, as we gave up witchcraft prosecutions about three hundred years ago, we don't like to have other people keeping on our discarded practices; it doesn't seem respectful to our mental and moral position."

"I hope you weren't unkind to the Bishop," said Annabel.

"Well, of course he was my guest, so I had to be outwardly polite to him, but he was tactless enough to rake up the incidents of the old quarrel, and to try to make out that there was something to be said for the way his side of the family had behaved; even if there was, which I don't for a moment admit, my house was not the place in which to say it. I didn't argue the matter, but I gave my cook a holiday to go and visit his aged parents some ninety miles away. The emergency cook was not a specialist in curries, in fact, I don't think cooking in any shape or form could have been one of his strong points. I believe he originally came to us in the guise of a gardener, but as we never pretended to have anything that could be considered a garden he was utilised as assistant goatherd, in which capacity, I understand, he gave every satisfaction. When the Bishop heard that I had sent away the cook on a special and unnecessary holiday he saw the inwardness of the manoeuvre, and from that moment we were scarcely on speaking terms. If you have ever had a Bishop with whom you were not on speaking terms staying in your house, you will appreciate the situation."

Annabel confessed that her life-story had never included such a disturbing experience.

"Then," continued Matilda, "to make matters more complicated, the Gwadlipichee overflowed its banks, a thing it did every now and then when the rains were unduly prolonged, and the lower part of the house and all the outbuildings were submerged. We managed to get the ponies loose in time, and the syce swam the whole lot of them off to the nearest rising ground. A goat or two, the chief goat-herd, the chief goat-herd's wife, and several of their babies came to anchorage in the verandah. All the rest of the available space was filled up with wet, bedraggled-looking hens and chickens; one never really knows how many fowls one possesses till the servants' quarters are flooded out. Of course, I had been through something of the sort in previous floods, but never before had I had a houseful of goats and babies and half-drowned hens, supplemented by a Bishop with whom I was hardly on speaking terms."

"It must have been a trying experience," commented Annabel.

"More embarrassments were to follow. I wasn't going to let a mere ordinary flood wash out the memory of that Crown Derby dessert service, and I intimated to the Bishop that his large bedroom, with a writing table in it, and his small bathroom, with a sufficiency of cold-water jars in it, was his share of the premises, and that space was rather congested under the existing circumstances. However, at about three o'clock in the afternoon, when he had awakened from his midday sleep, he made a sudden incursion into the room that was normally the drawing-room, but was now dining-room, storehouse, saddle-room, and half a dozen other temporary premises as well. From the condition of my guest's costume he seemed to think it might also serve as his dressing-room.

" 'I'm afraid there is nowhere for you to sit,' I said coldly; 'the verandah is full of goats.'

" 'There is a goat in my bedroom,' he observed with equal coldness, and more than a suspicion of sardonic reproach.

" 'Really,' I said, 'another survivor? I thought all the other goats were done for.'

" 'This particular goat is quite done for,' he said, 'it is being devoured by a leopard at the present moment. That is why I left the room; some animals resent being watched while they are eating.'

"The leopard, of course, was easily explained; it had been hanging round the goat sheds when the flood came, and had clambered up by the outside staircase leading to the Bishop's bathroom, thoughtfully bringing a goat with it. Probably it found the bathroom too damp and shut-in for its taste, and transferred its banqueting operations to the bedroom while the Bishop was having his nap."

"What a frightful situation!" exclaimed Annabel; "fancy having a ravening leopard in the house, with a flood all round you."

"Not in the least ravening," said Matilda; "it was full of goat, had any amount of water at its disposal if it felt thirsty, and probably had no more immediate wish than a desire for uninterrupted sleep. Still, I think any one will admit that it was an embarrassing predicament to have your only available guest-room occupied by a leopard, the verandah choked up with goats and babies and wet hens, and a Bishop with whom you were scarcely on speaking terms planted down in your own sitting-room. I really don't know how I got through those crawling hours, and of course mealtimes only made matters worse. The emergency cook had every excuse for sending in watery soup and sloppy rice, and as neither the chief goat-herd nor his wife were expert divers, the cellar could not be reached. Fortunately the Gwadlipichee subsides as rapidly as it rises, and just before dawn the syce came splashing back, with the ponies only fetlock deep in water. Then there arose some awkwardness from the fact that the Bishop wished to leave sooner than the leopard did, and as the latter was ensconced in the midst of the former's personal possessions there was an obvious difficulty in altering the order of departure. I pointed out to the Bishop that a leopard's habits and tastes are not those of an otter, and that it naturally preferred walking to wading; and that in any case a meal of an entire goat, washed down with tub-water, justified a certain amount of repose; if I had had guns fired to frighten the animal away, as the Bishop suggested, it would probably merely have left the bedroom to come into the already overcrowded drawing-room. Altogether it was rather a relief when they both left. Now, perhaps, you can understand my appreciation of a sleepy countryside where things don't happen."

THE PENANCE

OCTAVIAN RUTTLE was one of those lively cheerful individuals on whom amiability had set its unmistakable stamp, and, like most of his kind, his soul's peace depended in large measure on the unstinted approval of his fellows. In hunting to death a small tabby cat he had done a thing of which he scarcely approved himself, and he was glad when the gardener had hidden the body in its hastily dug grave under a lone oak tree in the meadow, the same tree that the hunted quarry had climbed as a last effort towards safety. It had been a distasteful and seemingly ruthless deed, but circumstances had demanded the doing of it. Octavian kept chickens; at least he kept some of them; others vanished from his keeping, leaving only a few bloodstained feathers to mark the manner of their going. The tabby cat from the large grey house that stood with its back to the meadow had been detected in many furtive visits to the hencoups, and after due negotiation with those in authority at the grey house a sentence of death had been agreed on. "The children will mind, but they need not know," had been the last word on the matter.

The children in question were a standing puzzle to Octavian; in the course of a few months he considered that he should have known their names, ages, the dates of their birthdays, and have been introduced to their favourite toys. They remained however, as noncommittal as the long blank wall that shut them off from the meadow, a wall over which their three heads sometimes appeared at odd moments. They had parents in India—that much Octavian had learned in the neighbourhood; the children, beyond grouping themselves garment-wise into sexes, a girl and two boys, carried their lifestory no further on his behoof. And now it seemed he was engaged in something which touched them closely, but must be hidden from their knowledge.

The poor helpless chickens had gone one by one to their doom, so it was meet that their destroyer should come to a violent end; yet Octavian felt some qualms when his share of the violence was ended. The little cat, headed off from its wonted tracks of safety, had raced unfriended from shelter to shelter, and its end had been rather piteous. Octavian walked through the long grass of the meadow with a step less jaunty than usual. And as he passed beneath the shadow of the high blank wall he glanced up and became aware that his hunting had had undesired witnesses. Three white set faces were looking down at him, and if ever an artist wanted a threefold study of cold human hate, impotent yet unyielding, raging yet masked in stillness, he would have found it in the triple gaze that met Octavian's eye.

"I'm sorry, but it had to be done," said Octavian, with genuine apology in his voice.

"Beast!"

The answer came from three throats with startling intensity.

Octavian felt that the blank wall would not be more impervious to his explanations than the bunch of human hostility that peered over its coping; he wisely decided to withhold his peace overtures till a more hopeful occasion.

Two days later he ransacked the best sweet shop in the neighbouring market town for a box of chocolates that by its size and contents should fitly atone for the dismal deed done under the oak tree in the meadow. The two first specimens that were shown him he hastily rejected; one had a group of chickens pictured on its lid, the other bore the portrait of a tabby kitten. A third sample was more simply bedecked with a spray of painted poppies, and Octavian hailed the flowers of forgetfulness as a happy omen. He felt distinctly more at ease with his surroundings when the imposing package had been sent across to the grey house, and a message returned to say that it had been duly given to the children. The next morning he sauntered with purposeful steps past the long blank wall on his way to the chicken-run and piggery that stood at the bottom of the meadow. The three children were perched at their accustomed lookout, and their range of sight did not seem to concern itself with Octavian's presence. As he became depressingly aware of the aloofness of their gaze he also noted a strange variegation in the herbage at his feet; the greensward for a considerable space around was strewn and speckled with a chocolate-coloured hail, enlivened here and there with gay tinsel-like wrappings or the glistening mauve of crystallised violets. It was as though the fairy paradise of a greedyminded child had taken shape and substance in the vegetation of the meadow. Octavian's bloodmoney had been flung back at him in scorn.

To increase his discomfiture, the march of events tended to shift the blame of ravaged chicken-coops from the supposed culprit who had already paid full forfeit; the young chicks were still carried off, and it seemed highly probable that the cat had only haunted the chicken-run to prey on the rats which harboured there. Through the flowing channels of servant talk the children learned of this belated revision of verdict, and Octavian one day picked up a sheet of copybook paper on which was painstakingly written: "Beast. Rats eated your chickens." More ardently than ever did he wish for an opportunity for sloughing off the disgrace that enwrapped him, and earning some happier nickname from his three unsparing judges.

And one day a chance inspiration came to him. Olivia, his two-year-old daughter, was accustomed to spend the hour from high noon till one o'clock with her father while the nursemaid gobbled and digested her dinner and novelette. About the same time the blank wall was usually enlivened by the presence of its three small wardens. Octavian, with seeming carelessness of purpose, brought Olivia well within hail of the watchers and noted with hidden delight the growing interest that dawned in that hitherto sternly hostile quarter. His little Olivia, with her sleepy placid ways, was going to succeed where he, with his anxious well-meant overtures, had so signally failed. He brought her a large yellow dahlia, which she grasped tightly in one hand and regarded with a stare of benevolent boredom, such as one might bestow on amateur classical dancing performed in aid of a deserving charity. Then he turned shyly to the group perched on the wall and asked with affected carelessness, "Do you like flowers?" Three solemn nods rewarded his venture.

"Which sorts do you like best?" he asked, this time with a distinct betrayal of eagerness in his voice.

"Those with all the colours, over there." Three chubby arms pointed to a distant tangle of sweetpea. Childlike, they had asked for what lay farthest from hand, but Octavian trotted off gleefully to obey their welcome behest. He pulled and plucked with unsparing hand, and brought every variety of tint that he could see into his bunch that was rapidly becoming a bundle. Then he turned to retrace his steps, and found the blank wall blanker and more deserted than ever, while the foreground was void of all trace of Olivia. Far down the meadow three children were pushing a go-cart at the utmost speed they could muster in the direction of the piggeries; it was Olivia's go-cart and Olivia sat in it, somewhat bumped and shaken by the pace at which she was being driven, but apparently retaining her wonted composure of mind. Octavian stared for a moment at the rapidly moving group, and then started in hot pursuit, shedding as he ran sprays of blossom from the mass of sweet-pea that he still clutched in his hands. Fast as he ran the children had reached the piggery before he could overtake them, and he arrived just in time to see Olivia, wondering but unprotesting, hauled and pushed up to the roof of the nearest sty. They were old buildings in some need of repair, and the rickety roof would certainly not have borne Octavian's weight if he had attempted to follow his daughter and her captors on their new vantage ground.

"What are you going to do with her?" he panted. There was no mistaking the grim trend of mischief in those flushed by sternly composed young faces.

"Hang her in chains over a slow fire," said one of the boys. Evidently they had been reading English history.

"Frow her down the pigs will d'vour her, every bit 'cept the palms of her hands," said the other boy. It was also evident that they had studied Biblical history.

The last proposal was the one which most alarmed Octavian, since it might be carried into effect at a moment's notice; there had been cases, he remembered, of pigs eating babies.

"You surely wouldn't treat my poor little Olivia in that way?" he pleaded.

"You killed our little cat," came in stern reminder from three throats.

"I'm sorry I did," said Octavian, and if there is a standard measurement in truths Octavian's statement was assuredly a large nine.

"We shall be very sorry when we've killed Olivia," said the girl, "but we can't be sorry till we've done it."

The inexorable child-logic rose like an unyielding rampart before Octavian's scared pleadings. Before he could think of any fresh line of appeal his energies were called out in another direction. Olivia had slid off the roof and fallen with a soft, unctuous splash into a morass of muck and decaying straw. Octavian scrambled hastily over the pigsty wall to her rescue, and at once found himself in a quagmire that engulfed his feet. Olivia, after the first shock of surprise at her sudden drop through the air, had been mildly pleased at finding herself in close and unstinted contact with the sticky element that oozed around her, but as she began to sink gently into the bed of slime a feeling dawned on her that she was not after all very happy, and she began to cry in the tentative fashion of the normally good child. Octavian, battling with the quagmire, which seemed to have learned the rare art of giving way at all points without yielding an inch, saw his daughter slowly disappearing in the engulfing slush, her smeared face further distorted with the contortions of whimpering wonder, while from their perch on the pigsty roof the three children looked down with the cold unpitying detachment of the Parcae Sisters.

"I can't reach her in time," gasped Octavian, "she'll be choked in the muck. Won't you help her?"

"No one helped our cat," came the inevitable reminder.

"I'll do anything to show you how sorry I am about that," cried Octavian, with a further desperate flounder, which carried him scarcely two inches forward.

"Will you stand in a white sheet by the grave?"

"Yes," screamed Octavian.

"Holding a candle?"

"An' saying 'I'm a miserable Beast'?"

Octavian agreed to both suggestions.

"For a long, long time?"

"For half an hour," said Octavian. There was an anxious ring in his voice as he named the time limit; was there not the precedent of a German king who did open-air penance for several days and nights at Christmas-time clad only in his shirt? Fortunately the children did not appear to have read German history, and half an hour seemed long and goodly in their eyes.

"All right," came with threefold solemnity from the roof, and a moment later a short ladder had been laboriously pushed across to Octavian, who lost no time in propping it against the low pigsty wall. Scrambling gingerly along its rungs he was able to lean across the morass that separated him from his slowly foundering offspring and extract her like an unwilling cork from it's slushy embrace. A few minutes later he was listening to the shrill and repeated assurances of the nursemaid that her previous experience of filthy spectacles had been on a notably smaller scale.

That same evening when twilight was deepening into darkness Octavian took up his position as penitent under the lone oak tree, having first carefully undressed the part. Clad in a zephyr shirt, which on this occasion thoroughly merited its name, he held in one hand a lighted candle and in the other a watch, into which the soul of a dead plumber seemed to have passed. A box of matches lay at his feet and was resorted to on the fairly frequent occasions when the candle succumbed to the night breezes. The house loomed inscrutable in the middle distance, but as Octavian conscientiously repeated the formula of his penance he felt certain that three pairs of solemn eyes were watching his moth-shared vigil.

And the next morning his eyes were gladdened by a sheet of copy-book paper lying beside the blank wall, on which was written the message, "Un-Beast."

THE PHANTOM LUNCHEON

"THE SMITHLY-DUBBS are in Town," said Sir James. "I wish you would show them some attention. Ask them to lunch with you at the Ritz or somewhere."

"From the little I've seen of the Smithly-Dubbs I don't thing I want to cultivate their acquaintance," said Lady Drakmanton.

"They always work for us at election times," said her husband; "I don't suppose they influence very many votes, but they have an uncle who is on one of my ward committees, and another uncle speaks sometimes at some of our less important meetings. Those sort of people expect some return in the shape of hospitality."

"Expect it!" exclaimed Lady Drakmanton; "the Misses Smithly-Dubb do more than that; they almost demand it. They belong to my club, and hang about the lobby just about lunch time, all three of them, with their tongues hanging out of their mouths and the six-course look in their eyes. If I were to breathe the word 'lunch' they would hustle me into a taxi and scream 'Ritz' or 'Dieudonne's' to the driver before I knew what was happening."

"All the same, I think you ought to ask them to a meal of some sort," persisted Sir James.

"I consider that showing hospitality to the Smithly-Dubbs is carrying Free Food principles to a regrettable extreme," said Lady Drakmanton; "I've entertained the Joneses and the Browns and the Snapheimers and the Lubrikoffs, and heaps of others whose names I forget, but I don't see why I should inflict the society of the Misses Smithly-Dubb on myself for a solid hour. Imagine it, sixty minutes, more or less, of unrelenting gobble and gabble. Why can't *you* take them on, Milly?" she asked, turning hopefully to her sister.

"I don't know them," said Milly hastily.

"All the better; you can pass yourself off as me. People say that we are so alike that they can hardly tell us apart, and I've only spoken to these tiresome young women about twice in my life, at committee-rooms, and bowed to them in the club. Any of the club page-boys will point them out to you; they're always to be found lolling about the hall just before lunch time."

"My dear Betty, don't be absurd," protested Milly; "I've got some people lunching with me at the Carlton tomorrow, and I'm leaving Town the day afterwards."

"What time is your lunch tomorrow?" asked Lady Drakmanton reflectively.

"Two o'clock," said Milly.

"Good," said her sister; "the Smithly-Dubbs shall lunch with me tomorrow. It shall be rather an amusing lunch party. At least, I shall be amused."

The last two remarks she made to herself. Other people did not always appreciate her ideas of humour. Sir James never did.

The next day Lady Drakmanton made some marked variations in her usual toilet effects. She dressed her hair in an unaccustomed manner, and put on a hat that added to the transformation of her appearance. When she had made one or two minor alterations she was sufficiently unlike her usual smart self to produce some hesitation in the greeting which the Misses Smithly-Dubb bestowed on her in the club lobby. She responded, however, with a readiness which set their doubts at rest.

"What is the Carlton like for lunching in?" she asked breezily.

The restaurant received an enthusiastic recommendation from the three sisters.

"Let's go and lunch there, shall we?" she suggested, and in a few minutes' time the Smithly-Dubb mind was contemplating at close quarters a happy vista of baked meats and approved vintage.

"Are you going to start with caviare? I am," confided Lady Drakmanton, and the Smithly-Dubbs started with caviare. The subsequent dishes were chosen in the same ambitious spirit, and by the time they had arrived at the wild duck course it was beginning to be a rather expensive lunch.

The conversation hardly kept pace with the brilliancy of the menu. Repeated references on the part of the guests to the local political conditions and prospects in Sir James's constituency were met with vague "ahs" and "indeeds" from Lady Drakmanton, who might have been expected to be specially interested.

"I think when the Insurance Act is a little better understood it will lose some of its present unpopularity," hazarded Cecilia Smithly-Dubb.

"Will it? I dare say. I'm afraid politics don't interest me very much," said Lady Drakmanton.

The three Miss Smithly-Dubbs put down their cups of Turkish coffee and stared. Then they broke into protesting giggles.

"Of course, you're joking," they said.

"Not me," was the disconcerting answer; "I can't make head or tail of these bothering old politics. Never could, and never want to. I've quite enough to do to manage my own affairs, and that's a fact."

"But," exclaimed Amanda Smithly-Dubb, with a squeal of bewilderment breaking into her voice, "I was told you spoke so informingly about the Insurance Act at one of our social evenings."

It was Lady Drakmanton who stared now. "Do you know," she said, with a scared look around her, "rather a dreadful thing is happening. I'm suffering from a complete loss of memory. I can't even think who I am. I remember meeting you somewhere, and I remember you asking me to come and lunch with you here, and that I accepted your kind invitation. Beyond that my mind is a positive blank."

The scared look was transferred with intensified poignancy to the faces of her companions.

"*You* asked *us* to lunch," they exclaimed hurriedly. That seemed a more immediately important point to clear up than the question of identity.

"Oh, no," said the vanishing hostess, "*that* I do remember about. You insisted on my coming here because the feeding was so good, and I must say it comes up to all you said about it. A very nice lunch it's been. What I'm worrying about is who on earth am I? I haven't the faintest notion?"

"You are Lady Drakmanton," exclaimed the three sisters in chorus.

"Now, don't make fun of me," she replied, crossly, "I happen to know her quite well by sight, and she isn't a bit like me. And it's an odd thing you should have mentioned her, for it so happens she's just come into the room. That lady in black, with the yellow plume in her hat, there over by the door."

The Smithly-Dubbs looked in the indicated direction, and the uneasiness in their eyes deepened into horror. In outward appearance the lady who had just entered the room certainly came rather nearer to their recollection of their Member's wife than the individual who was sitting at table with them.

"Who *are* you, then, if that is Lady Drakmanton?" they asked in panic-stricken bewilderment.

"That is just what I don't know," was the answer; "and you don't seem to know much better than I do."

"You came up to us in the club—"

"In what club?"

"The New Didactic, in Calais Street."

"The New Didactic!" exclaimed Lady Drakmanton with an air of returning illumination; "thank you so much. Of course, I remember now who I am. I'm Ellen Niggle, of the Ladies' Brasspolishing Guild. The Club employs me to come now and then and see to the polishing of the brass fittings. That's how I came to know Lady Drakmanton by sight; she's very often in the Club. And you are the ladies who so kindly asked me out to lunch. Funny how it should all have slipped my memory, all of a sudden. The unaccustomed good food and wine must have been too much for me; for the moment I really couldn't call to mind who I was. Good gracious," she broke off suddenly, "it's ten past two; I should be at a polishing job in Whitehall. I must scuttle off like a giddy rabbit. Thanking you ever so."

She left the room with a scuttle sufficiently suggestive of the animal she had mentioned, but the giddiness was all on the side of her involuntary hostesses. The restaurant seemed to be spinning round them; and the bill when it appeared did nothing to restore their composure. They were as nearly in tears as it is permissible to be during the luncheon hour in a really good restaurant. Financially speaking, they were well able to afford the luxury of an elaborate lunch, but their ideas on the subject of entertaining differed very sharply, according to the circumstances of whether they were dispensing or receiving hospitality. To have fed themselves liberally at their own expense was, perhaps, an extravagance to be deplored, but, at any rate, they had had something for their money; to have drawn an unknown and socially unremunerative Ellen Niggle into the net of their hospitality was a catastrophe that they could not contemplate with any degree of calmness.

The Smithly-Dubbs never quite recovered from their unnerving experience. They have given up politics and taken to doing good.

A BREAD AND BUTTER MISS

"STARLING CHATTER and Oakhill have both dropped back in the betting," said Bertie van Tahn, throwing the morning paper across the breakfast table.

"That leaves Nursery Tea practically favourite," said Odo Finsberry.

"Nursery Tea and Pipeclay are at the top of the betting at present," said Bertie, "but that French horse, Le Five O'Clock, seems to be fancied as much as anything. Then there is Whitebait, and the Polish horse with a name like some one trying to stifle a sneeze in church; they both seem to have a lot of support."

"It's the most open Derby there's been for years," said Odo.

"It's simply no good trying to pick the winner on form," said Bertie; "one must just trust to luck and inspiration."

"The question is whether to trust to one's own inspiration, or somebody else's. Sporting Swank gives Count Palatine to win, and Le Five O'Clock for a place."

"Count Palatine—that adds another to our list of perplexities. Good morning, Sir Lulworth; have you a fancy for the Derby by any chance?"

"I don't usually take much interest in turf matters," said Sir Lulworth, who had just made his appearance, "but I always like to have a bet on the Guineas and the Derby. This year, I confess, it's rather difficult to pick out anything that seems markedly better than anything else. What do you think of Snow Bunting?"

"Snow Bunting?" said Odo, with a groan, "there's another of them. Surely, Snow Bunting has no earthly chance?"

"My housekeeper's nephew, who is a shoeing-smith in the mounted section of the Church Lads' Brigade, and an authority on horseflesh, expects him to be among the first three."

"The nephews of housekeepers are invariably optimists," said Bertie; "it's a kind of natural reaction against the professional pessimism of their aunts."

"We don't seem to get much further in our search for the probable winner," said Mrs. de Claux; "the more I listen to you experts the more hopelessly befogged I get."

"It's all very well to blame us," said Bertie to his hostess; "you haven't produced anything in the way of an inspiration."

"My inspiration consisted in asking you down for Derby week," retorted Mrs. de Claux; "I thought you and Odo between you might throw some light on the question of the moment."

Further recriminations were cut short by the arrival of Lola Pevensey, who floated into the room with an air of gracious apology.

"So sorry to be so late," she observed, making a rapid tour of inspection of the breakfast dishes.

"Did you have a good night?" asked her hostess with perfunctory solicitude.

"Quite, thank you," said Lola; "I dreamt a most remarkable dream."

A flutter, indicative of general boredom; went round the table. Other people's dreams are about as universally interesting as accounts of other people's gardens, or chickens, or children.

"I dreamt about the winner of the Derby," said Lola.

A swift reaction of attentive interest set in.

"Do tell us what you dreamt," came in a chorus.

"The really remarkable thing about it is that I've dreamt it two nights running," said Lola, finally deciding between the allurements of sausages and kedgeree; "that is why I thought it worth mentioning. You know, when I dream things two or three nights in succession, it always means something; I have special powers in that way. For instance, I once dreamed three times that a winged lion was flying through the sky and one of his wings dropped off, and he came to the ground with a crash; just afterwards the Campanile at Venice fell down. The winged lion is the symbol of Venice, you know," she added for the enlightenment of those who might not be versed in Italian heraldry. "Then," she continued, "just before the murder of the King and Queen of Servia I had a vivid dream of two crowned figures walking into a slaughterhouse by the banks of a big river, which I took to be the Danube; and only the other day—"

"Do tell us what you've dreamt about the Derby," interrupted Odo impatiently.

"Well, I saw the finish of the race as clearly as anything; and one horse won easily, almost in a canter, and everybody cried out 'Bread and Butter wins! Good old Bread and Butter.' I heard the name distinctly, and I've had the same dream two nights running."

"Bread and Butter," said Mrs. de Claux, "now, whatever horse can that point to? Why—of course; Nursery Tea!"

She looked round with the triumphant smile of a successful unraveller of mystery.

"How about Le Five O'Clock?" interposed Sir Lulworth.

"It would fit either of them equally well," said Odo; "can you remember any details about the jockey's colours? That might help us."

"I seem to remember a glimpse of lemon sleeves or cap, but I can't be sure," said Lola, after due reflection.

"There isn't a lemon jacket or cap in the race," said Bertie, referring to a list of starters and jockeys; "can't you remember anything about the appearance of the horse? If it were a thick-set animal, this bread and butter would typify Nursery Tea; and if it were thin, of course, it would mean Le Five O'Clock."

"That seems sound enough," said Mrs. de Claux; "do think, Lola dear, whether the horse in your dream was thin or stoutly built."

"I can't remember that it was one or the other," said Lola; "one wouldn't notice such a detail in the excitement of a finish."

"But this was a symbolic animal," said Sir Lulworth; "if it were to typify thick or thin bread and butter surely it ought to have been either as bulky and tubby as a shire cart-horse; or as thin as a heraldic leopard."

"I'm afraid you are rather a careless dreamer," said Bertie resentfully.

"Of course, at the moment of dreaming I thought I was witnessing a real race, not the portent of one," said Lola; "otherwise I should have particularly noticed all helpful details."

"The Derby isn't run till tomorrow," said Mrs. de Claux; "do you think you are likely to have the same dream again tonight? If so; you can fix your attention on the important detail of the animal's appearance."

"I'm afraid I shan't sleep at all tonight," said Lola pathetically; "every fifth night I suffer from insomnia, and it's due tonight."

"It's most provoking," said Bertie; "of course, we can back both horses, but it would be much more satisfactory to have all our money on the winner. Can't you take a sleeping-draught, or something?"

"Oakleaves, soaked in warm water and put under the bed, are recommended by some," said Mrs. de Claux.

"A glass of Benedictine, with a drop of eau-de-Cologne—" said Sir Lulworth.

"I have tried every known remedy," said Lola, with dignity; "I've been a martyr to insomnia for years."

"But now we are being martyrs to it," said Odo sulkily; "I particularly want to land a big coup over this race."

"I don't have insomnia for my own amusement," snapped Lola.

"Let us hope for the best," said Mrs. de Claux soothingly; "tonight may prove an exception to the fifth-night rule."

But when breakfast time came round again Lola reported a blank night as far as visions were concerned.

"I don't suppose I had as much as ten minutes' sleep, and, certainly, no dreams."

"I'm so sorry, for your sake in the first place, and ours as well," said her hostess; "do you think you could induce a short nap after breakfast? It would be so good for you—and you *might* dream something. There would still be time for us to get our bets on."

"I'll try if you like," said Lola; "it sounds rather like a small child being sent to bed in disgrace."

"I'll come and read the Encyclopaedia Britannica to you if you think it will make you sleep any sooner," said Bertie obligingly.

Rain was falling too steadily to permit of outdoor amusement, and the party suffered considerably during the next two hours from the absolute quiet that was enforced all over the house in order to give Lola every chance of achieving slumber. Even the click of billiard balls was considered a possible factor of disturbance, and the canaries were carried down to the gardener's lodge, while the cuckoo clock in the hall was muffled under several layers of rugs. A notice, "Please do not Knock or Ring," was posted on the front door at Bertie's suggestion, and guests and servants spoke in tragic whispers as though the dread presence of death or sickness had invaded the house. The precautions proved of no avail: Lola added a sleepless morning to a wakeful night, and the bets of the party had to be impartially divided between Nursery Tea and the French Colt.

"So provoking to have to split out bets," said Mrs. de Claux, as her guests gathered in the hall later in the day, waiting for the result of the race.

"I did my best for you," said Lola, feeling that she was not getting her due share of gratitude; "I told you what I had seen in my dreams, a brown horse, called Bread and Butter, winning easily from all the rest."

"What?" screamed Bertie, jumping up from his sea, "a brown horse! Miserable woman, you never said a word about it's being a brown horse."

"Didn't I?" faltered Lola; "I thought I told you it was a brown horse. It was certainly brown in both dreams. But I don't see what the colour has got to do with it. Nursery Tea and Le Five O'Clock are both chestnuts."

"Merciful Heaven! Doesn't brown bread and butter with a sprinkling of lemon in the colours suggest anything to you?" raged Bertie.

A slow, cumulative groan broke from the assembly as the meaning of his words gradually dawned on his hearers.

For the second time that day Lola retired to the seclusion of her room; she could not face the universal looks of reproach directed at her when Whitebait was announced winner at the comfortable price of fourteen to one.

BERTIE'S CHRISTMAS EVE

IT WAS Christmas Eve, and the family circle of Luke Steffink, Esq., was aglow with the amiability and random mirth which the occasion demanded. A long and lavish dinner had been partaken of, waits had been round and sung carols; the house-party had regaled itself with more caroling on its own account, and there had been romping which, even in a pulpit reference, could not have been condemned as ragging. In the midst of the general glow, however, there was one black unkindled cinder.

Bertie Steffink, nephew of the aforementioned Luke, had early in life adopted the profession of ne'er-do-well; his father had been something of the kind before him. At the age of eighteen Bertie had commenced that round of visits to our Colonial possessions, so seemly and desirable in the case of a Prince of the Blood, so suggestive of insincerity in a young man of the middle-class. He had gone to grow tea in Ceylon and fruit in British Columbia, and to help sheep to grow wool in Australia. At the age of twenty he had just returned from some similar errand in Canada, from which it may be gathered that the trial he gave to these various experiments was of the summary drum-head nature. Luke Steffink, who fulfilled the troubled role of guardian and deputy-parent to Bertie, deplored the persistent manifestation of the homing instinct on his nephew's part, and his solemn thanks earlier in the day for the blessing of reporting a united family had no reference to Bertie's return.

Arrangements had been promptly made for packing the youth off to a distant corner of Rhodesia, whence return would be a difficult matter; the journey to this uninviting destination was imminent, in fact a more careful and willing traveller would have already begun to think about his packing. Hence Bertie was in no mood to share in the festive spirit which displayed itself around him, and resentment smouldered within him at the eager, self-absorbed discussion of social plans for the coming months which he heard on all sides. Beyond depressing his uncle and the family circle generally by singing "Say au revoir, and not good-bye," he had taken no part in the evening's conviviality.

Eleven o'clock had struck some half-hour ago, and the elder Steffinks began to throw out suggestions leading up to that process which they called retiring for the night.

"Come, Teddie, it's time you were in your little bed, you know," said Luke Steffink to his thirteen-year-old son.

"That's where we all ought to be," said Mrs. Steffink.

"There wouldn't be room," said Bertie.

The remark was considered to border on the scandalous; everybody ate raisins and almonds with the nervous industry of sheep feeding during threatening weather.

"In Russia," said Horace Bordenby, who was staying in the house as a Christmas guest, "I've read that the peasants believe that if you go into a cow-house or stable at midnight on Christmas Eve you will hear the animals talk. They're supposed to have the gift of speech at that one moment of the year."

"Oh, *do* let's *all* go down to the cow-house and listen to what they've got to say!" exclaimed Beryl, to whom anything was thrilling and amusing if you did it in a troop.

Mrs. Steffink made a laughing protest, but gave a virtual consent by saying, "We must all wrap up well, then." The idea seemed a scatter-brained one to her, and almost heathenish, but if afforded an opportunity for "throwing the young people together," and as such she welcomed it. Mr. Horace Bordenby was a young man with quite substantial prospects, and he had danced with Beryl at a local subscription ball a sufficient number of times to warrant the authorised inquiry on the part of the neighbours whether "there was anything in it." Though Mrs. Steffink would not have put it in so many words, she shared the idea of the Russian peasantry that on this night the beast might speak.

The cow-house stood at the junction of the garden with a small paddock, an isolated survival, in a suburban neighbourhood; of what had once been a small farm. Luke Steffink was complacently proud of his cow-house and his two cows; he felt that they gave him a stamp of solidity which no number of Wyandottes or Orpingtons could impart. They

even seemed to link him in a sort of inconsequent way with those patri-
archs who derived importance from their floating capital of flocks and
herbs, he-asses and she-asses. It had been an anxious and momentous occasion when he had had to decide definitely between "the Byre" and "the
Ranch" for the naming of his villa residence. A December midnight was
hardly the moment he would have chosen for showing his farm-building
to visitors, but since it was a fine night, and the young people were anxious for an excuse for a mild frolic, Luke consented to chaperon the expedition. The servants had long since gone to bed, so the house was left
in charge of Bertie, who scornfully declined to stir out on the pretext of
listening to bovine conversation.

"We must go quietly," said Luke, as he headed the procession of gig-
gling young folk, brought up in the rear by the shawled and hooded figure of Mrs. Steffink; "I've always laid stress on keeping this a quiet and
orderly neighbourhood."

It was a few minutes to midnight when the party reached the cow-
house and made its way in by the light of Luke's stable lantern. For a moment every one stood in silence, almost with a feeling of being in church.

"Daisy—the one lying down—is by a shorthorn bull out of a Guern-
sey cow," announced Luke in a hushed voice, which was in keeping with
the foregoing impression.

"Is she?" said Bordenby, rather as if he had expected her to be by
Rembrandt.

"Myrtle is—"

Myrtle's family history was cut short by a little scream from the
women of the party.

The cow-house door had closed noiselessly behind them and the key
had turned gratingly in the lock; then they heard Bertie's voice pleasantly wishing them good-night and his footsteps retreating along the garden path.

Luke Steffink strode to the window; it was a small square opening of
the old-fashioned sort, with iron bars let into the stonework.

"Unlock the door this instant," he shouted, with as much air of
menacing authority as a hen might assume when screaming through the

bars of a coop at a marauding hawk. In reply to his summons the hall door closed with a defiant bang.

A neighbouring clock struck the hour of midnight. If the cows had received the gift of human speech at that moment they would not have been able to make themselves heard. Seven or eight other voices were engaged in describing Bertie's present conduct and his general character at a high pressure of excitement and indignation.

In the course of half an hour or so everything that it was permissible to say about Bertie had been said some dozens of times, and other topics began to come to the front—the extreme mustiness of the cow-house, the possibility of it catching fire, and the probability of it being a Rowton House for the vagrant rats of the neighbourhood. And still no sign of deliverance came to the unwilling vigil-keepers.

Towards one o'clock the sound of rather boisterous and undisciplined carol-singing approached rapidly, and came to a sudden anchorage, apparently just outside the garden gate. A motor-load of youthful "bloods," in a high state of conviviality, had made a temporary halt for repairs; the stoppage, however, did not extend to the vocal efforts of the party, and the watchers in the cow-shed were treated to a highly unauthorised rendering of "Good King Wenceslas," in which the adjective "good" appeared to be very carelessly applied.

The noise had the effect of bringing Bertie out into the garden, but he utterly ignored the pale, angry faces peering out at the cow-house window, and concentrated his attention on the revellers outside the gate.

"Wassail, you chaps!" he shouted.

"Wassail, old sport!" they shouted back; "we'd jolly well drink y'r health, only we've nothing to drink it in."

"Come and wassail inside," said Bertie hospitably; "I'm all alone, and there's heap's of 'wet'."

They were total strangers, but his touch of kindness made them instantly his kin. In another moment the unauthorised version of King Wenceslas, which, like many other scandals, grew worse on repetition, went echoing up the garden path; two of the revellers gave an impromptu performance on the way by executing the staircase waltz up the terraces of what Luke Steffink, hitherto with some justification, called his rock garden. The rock part of it was still there when the waltz had been accorded its third encore. Luke, more than ever like a cooped hen behind the cow-house bars, was in a position to realise the feelings of concert-goers unable to countermand the call for an encore which they neither desire or deserve.

The hall door closed with a bang on Bertie's guests, and the sounds of merriment became faint and muffled to the weary watchers at the other end of the garden. Presently two ominous pops, in quick succession, made themselves distinctly heard.

"They've got at the champagne!" exclaimed Mrs. Steffink.

"Perhaps it's the sparkling Moselle," said Luke hopefully.

Three or four more pops were heard.

"The champagne and the sparkling Moselle," said Mrs. Steffink.

Luke uncorked an expletive which, like brandy in a temperance household, was only used on rare emergencies. Mr. Horace Bordenby had been making use of similar expressions under his breath for a considerable time past. The experiment of "throwing the young people together" had been prolonged beyond a point when it was likely to produce any romantic result.

Some forty minutes later the hall door opened and disgorged a crowd that had thrown off any restraint of shyness that might have influenced its earlier actions. Its vocal efforts in the direction of carol singing were now supplemented by instrumental music; a Christmas tree that had been prepared for the children of the gardener and other household retainers had yielded a rich spoil of tin trumpets, rattles, and drums. The life story of King Wenceslas had been dropped, Luke was thankful to notice, but it was intensely irritating for the chilled prisoners in the cow-house to be told that it was a hot time in the old town tonight, together with some accurate but entirely superfluous information as to the imminence of Christmas morning. Judging by the protests which began to be shouted from the upper windows of neighbouring houses the sentiments prevailing in the cow-house were heartily echoed in other quarters.

The revellers found their car, and, what was more remarkable, managed to drive off in it, with a parting fanfare of tin trumpets. The lively beat of a drum disclosed the fact that the master of the revels remained on the scene.

"Bertie!" came in an angry, imploring chorus of shouts and screams from the cow-house window.

"Hullo," cried the owner of the name, turning his rather errant steps in the direction of the summons; "are you people still there? Must have heard everything cows got to say by this time. If you haven't, no use waiting. After all, it's a Russian legend, and Russian Chrismush Eve not due for 'nother fortnight. Better come out."

After one or two ineffectual attempts he managed to pitch the key of the cow-house door in through the window. Then, lifting his voice in the strains of "I'm afraid to go home in the dark," with a lusty drum accompaniment, he led the way back to the house. The hurried procession of the released that followed in his steps came in for a good deal of the adverse comment that his exuberant display had evoked.

It was the happiest Christmas Eve he had ever spent. To quote his own words, he had a rotten Christmas.

FOREWARNED

ALETHIA DEBCHANCE sat in a corner of an otherwise empty railway carriage, more or less at ease as regarded body, but in some trepidation as to mind. She had embarked on a social adventure of no little magnitude as compared with the accustomed seclusion and stagnation of her past life. At the age of twenty-eight she could look back on nothing more eventful than the daily round of her existence in her aunt's house at Webblehinton, a hamlet four and a half miles distant from a country town and about a quarter of a century removed from modern times. Their neighbours had been elderly and few, not much given to social intercourse, but helpful or politely sympathetic in times of illness. Newspapers of the ordinary kind were a rarity; those that Alethia saw regularly were devoted exclusively either to religion or to poultry, and the world of politics was to her an unheeded unexplored region. Her ideas on life in general had been acquired through the medium of popular respectable novel-writers, and modified or emphasised by such knowledge as her aunt, the vicar, and her aunt's housekeeper had put at her disposal. And now, in her twenty-ninth year, her aunt's death had left her, well provided for as regards income, but somewhat isolated in the matter of kith and kin and human companionship. She had some cousins who were on terms of friendly, though infrequent, correspondence with her, but as they lived permanently in Ceylon, a locality about which she knew little, beyond the assurance contained in the missionary hymn that the human element there was vile, they were not of much immediate use to her. Other cousins she also possessed, more distant as regards relationship, but not quite so geographically remote, seeing that they lived somewhere in the Midlands. She could hardly remember ever having met them, but once or twice in the course of the last three or four years they had expressed a polite wish that she should pay them a visit; they had probably not been unduly depressed by the fact that her aunt's failing health had prevented her from accepting their invitation. The note of condolence that had arrived on the occasion of her aunt's death had included a vague hope that Alethia would find time in the near future to spend a few days with her cousins, and after much deliberation and many hesitations she had written to propose herself as a guest for a definite date some week ahead. The family, she reflected with relief, was not a large one; the two daughters were married and away, there was only old Mrs. Bludward and her son Robert at home. Mrs. Bludward was something of an invalid, and Robert was a young man who had been at Oxford and was going into Parliament. Further than that Alethia's information did not go; her imagination, founded on her extensive knowledge of the people one met in novels, had to supply the gaps. The mother was not difficult to place; she would either be an ultra-amiable old lady, bearing her feeble health with uncomplaining fortitude, and having a kind word for the gardener's boy and a sunny smile for the chance visitor, or else she would be cold and peevish, with eyes that pierced you like a gimlet, and a unreasoning idolatry of her son. Alethia's imagination rather inclined her to the latter view. Robert was more of a problem. There were three dominant types of manhood to be taken into consideration in working out his classification; there was Hugo, who was strong, good, and beautiful, a rare type and not very often met with; there was Sir Jasper, who was utterly vile and absolutely unscrupulous, and there was Nevil, who was not really bad at heart, but had a weak mouth and usually required the life-work of two good women to keep him from ultimate disaster. It was probable, Alethia considered, that Robert came into the last category, in which case she was certain to enjoy the companionship of one or two excellent women, and might possibly catch glimpses of undesirable adventuresses or come face to face with reckless admiration-seeking married women. It was altogether an exciting prospect, this sudden venture into an unexplored world of unknown human beings, and Alethia rather wished that she could have taken the vicar with her; she was not, however, rich or important enough to travel with a chaplain, as the Marquis of Moystoncleugh always did in the novel she had just been reading, so she recognised that such a proceeding was out of the question.

The train which carried Alethia towards her destination was a local one, with the wayside station habit strongly developed. At most of the stations no one seemed to want to get into the train or to leave it, but at one there were several market folk on the platform, and two men, of the farmer or small cattle-dealer class, entered Alethia's carriage. Apparently they had just foregathered, after a day's business, and their conversation consisted of a rapid exchange of short friendly inquiries as to health, family, stock, and so forth, and some grumbling remarks on the weather. Suddenly, however, their talk took a dramatically interesting turn, and Alethia listened with wide-eyed attention.

"What do you think of Mister Robert Bludward, eh?"

There was a certain scornful ring in his question.

"Robert Bludward? An out-an'-out rotter, that's what he is. Ought to be ashamed to look any decent man in the face. Send him to Parliament to represent us—not much! He'd rob a poor man of his last shilling, he would."

"Ah, that he would. Tells a pack of lies to get our votes, that's all that he's after, damn him. Did you see the way the Argus showed him up this week? Properly exposed him, hip and thigh, I tell you."

And so on they ran, in their withering indictment. There could be no doubt that it was Alethia's cousin and prospective host to whom they were referring; the allusion to a Parliamentary candidature settled that. What could Robert Bludward have done, what manner of man could he be, that people should speak of him with such obvious reprobation?

"He was hissed down at Shoalford yesterday," said one of the speakers.

Hissed! Had it come to that? There was something dramatically biblical in the idea of Robert Bludward's neighbours and acquaintances hissing him for very scorn. Lord Hereward Stranglath had been hissed, now Alethia came to think of it, in the eighth chapter of Matterby Towers, while in the act of opening a Wesleyan bazaar, because he was suspected (unjustly as it turned out afterwards) of having beaten the German governess to death. And in Tainted Guineas Roper Squenderby had been deservedly hissed, on the steps of the Jockey Club, for having handed a rival owner a forged telegram, containing false news of his mother's death, just before the start for an important race, thereby ensuring the withdrawal of his rival's horse. In placid Saxon-blooded England people did not demonstrate their feelings lightly and without some strong compelling cause. What manner of evildoer was Robert Bludward?

The train stopped at another small station, and the two men got out. One of them left behind him a copy of the Argus, the local paper to which he had made reference. Alethia pounced on it, in the expectation of finding a cultured literary endorsement of the censure which these rough farming men had expressed in their homely, honest way. She had not far to look; "Mr. Robert Bludward, Swanker," was the title of one of the principal articles in the paper. She did not exactly know what a swanker was, probably it referred to some unspeakable form of cruelty, but she read enough in the first few sentences of the article to discover that her cousin Robert, the man at whose house she was about to stay, was an unscrupulous, unprincipled character, of a low order of intelligence, yet cunning withal, and that he and his associates were responsible for most of the misery, disease, poverty, and ignorance with which the country was afflicted; never, except in one or two of the denunciatory Psalms, which she had always supposed to have be written in a spirit of exaggerated Oriental imagery, had she read such an indictment of a human being. And this monster was going to meet her at Derrelton Station in a few short minutes. She would know him at once; he would have the dark beetling brows, the quick, furtive glance, the sneering, unsavoury smile that always characterised the Sir Jaspers of this world. It was too late to escape; she must force herself to meet him with outward calm.

It was a considerable shock to her to find that Robert was fair, with a snub nose, merry eye, and rather a schoolboy manner. "A serpent in duckling's plumage," was her private comment; merciful chance had revealed him to her in his true colours.

As they drove away from the station a dissipated-looking man of the labouring class waved his hat in friendly salute. "Good luck to you, Mr. Bludward," he shouted; "you'll come out on top! We'll break old Chobham's neck for him."

"Who was that man?" asked Alethia quickly.

"Oh, one of my supporters," laughed Robert; "a bit of a poacher and a bit of a pub-loafer, but he's on the right side."

So these were the sort of associates that Robert Bludward consorted with, thought Alethia.

"Who is the person he referred to as old Chobham?" she asked.

"Sir John Chobham, the man who is opposing me," answered Robert; "that is his house away there among the trees on the right."

So there was an upright man, possibly a very Hugo in character, who was thwarting and defying the evildoer in his nefarious career, and there was a dastardly plot afoot to break his neck! Possibly the attempt would be made within the next few hours. He must certainly be warned. Alethia remembered how Lady Sylvia Broomgate, in Nightshade Court, had pretended to be bolted with by her horse up to the front door of a threatened county magnate, and had whispered a warning in his ear which saved him from being the victim of foul murder. She wondered if there was a quiet pony in the stables on which she would be allowed to ride out alone. The chances were that she would be watched. Robert would come spurring after her and seize her bridle just as she was turning in at Sir John's gates.

A group of men that they passed in a village street gave them no very friendly looks, and Alethia thought she heard a furtive hiss; a moment later they came upon an errand boy riding a bicycle. He had the frank open countenance, neatly brushed hair and tidy clothes that betoken a clear conscience and a good mother. He stared straight at the occupants of the car, and, after he had passed them, sang in his clear, boyish voice:

"We'll hang Bobby Bludward on the sour apple tree."

Robert merely laughed. That was how he took the scorn and condemnation of his fellow-men. He had goaded them to desperation with his shameless depravity till they spoke openly of putting him to a violent death, and he laughed.

Mrs. Bludward proved to be of the type that Alethia had suspected, thin-lipped, cold-eyed, and obviously devoted to her worthless son. From her no help was to be expected. Alethia locked her door that night, and placed such ramparts of furniture against it that the maid had great difficulty in breaking in with the early tea in the morning.

After breakfast Alethia, on the pretext of going to look at an outlying rose-garden, slipped away to the village through which they had passed on the previous evening. She remembered that Robert had pointed out to her a public reading-room, and here she considered it possible that she might meet Sir John Chobham, or some one who knew him well and would carry a message to him. The room was empty when she entered it; a Graphic twelve days old, a yet older copy of Punch, and one or two local papers lay upon the central table; the other tables were stacked for the most part with chess and draughts-boards, and wooden boxes of chessmen and dominoes. Listlessly she picked up one of the papers, the Sentinel, and glanced at its contents. Suddenly she started, and began to read with breathless attention a prominently printed article, headed "A Little Limelight on Sir John Chobham." The colour ebbed away from her face, a look of frightened despair crept into her eyes. Never, in any novel that she had read, had a defenceless young woman been confronted with a situation like this. Sir John, the Hugo of her imagination, was, if anything, rather more depraved and despicable than Robert Bludward. He was mean, evasive, callously indifferent to his country's interests, a cheat, a man who habitually broke his word, and who was responsible, with his associates, for most of the poverty, misery, crime, and national degradation with which the country was afflicted. He was also a candidate for Parliament, it seemed, and as there was only one seat in this particular locality, it was obvious that the success of either Robert or Sir John would mean a check to the ambitions of the other, hence, no doubt, the rivalry and enmity between these otherwise kindred souls. One was seeking to have his enemy done to death, the other was apparently trying to stir up his supporters to an act of "Lynch law". All this in order that there might be an unopposed election, that one or other of the candidates might go into Parliament with honeyed eloquence on his lips and blood on his heart. Were men really so vile?

"I must go back to Webblehinton at once," Alethia informed her astonished hostess at lunch time; "I have had a telegram. A friend is very seriously ill and I have been sent for."

It was dreadful to have to concoct lies, but it would be more dreadful to have to spend another night under that roof.

Alethia reads novels now with even greater appreciation than before. She has been herself in the world outside Webblehinton, the world where the great dramas of sin and villainy are played unceasingly. She had come unscathed through it, but what might have happened if she had gone unsuspectingly to visit Sir John Chobham and warn him of his danger? What indeed! She had been saved by the fearless outspokenness of the local Press.

THE INTERLOPERS

IN A forest of mixed growth somewhere on the eastern spurs of the Karpathians, a man stood one winter night watching and listening, as though he waited for some beast of the woods to come within the range of his vision, and, later, of his rifle. But the game for whose presence he kept so keen an outlook was none that figured in the sportsman's calendar as lawful and proper for the chase; Ulrich von Gradwitz patrolled the dark forest in quest of a human enemy.

The forest lands of Gradwitz were of wide extent and well stocked with game; the narrow strip of precipitous woodland that lay on its outskirt was not remarkable for the game it harboured or the shooting it afforded, but it was the most jealously guarded of all its owner's territorial possessions. A famous law suit, in the days of his grandfather, had wrested it from the illegal possession of a neighbouring family of petty landowners; the dispossessed party had never acquiesced in the judgment of the Courts, and a long series of poaching affrays and similar scandals had embittered the relationships between the families for three generations. The neighbour feud had grown into a personal one since Ulrich had come to be head of his family; if there was a man in the world whom he detested and wished ill to it was Georg Znaeym, the inheritor of the quarrel and the tireless game-snatcher and raider of the disputed border-forest. The feud might, perhaps, have died down or been compromised if the personal ill-will of the two men had not stood in the way; as boys they had thirsted for one another's blood, as men each prayed that misfortune might fall on the other, and this wind-scourged winter night Ulrich had banded together his foresters to watch the dark forest, not in quest of four-footed quarry, but to keep a lookout for the prowling thieves whom he suspected of being afoot from across the land boundary. The roebuck, which usually kept in the sheltered hollows during a storm-wind, were running like driven things tonight, and there was movement and unrest among the creatures that were wont to sleep through the dark hours. Assuredly there was a disturbing element in the forest, and Ulrich could guess the quarter from whence it came.

He strayed away by himself from the watchers whom he had placed in ambush on the crest of the hill, and wandered far down the steep slopes amid the wild tangle of undergrowth, peering through the tree trunks and listening through the whistling and skirling of the wind and the restless beating of the branches for sight and sound of the marauders. If only on this wild night, in this dark, lone spot, he might come across Georg Znaeym, man to man, with none to witness— that was the wish that was uppermost in his thoughts. And as he stepped round the trunk of a huge beech he came face to face with the man he sought.

The two enemies stood glaring at one another for a long silent moment. Each had a rifle in his hand, each had hate in his heart and murder uppermost in his mind. The chance had come to give full play to the passions of a lifetime. But a man who has been brought up under the code of a restraining civilisation cannot easily nerve himself to shoot down his neighbour in cold blood and without word spoken, except for an offence against his hearth and honour. And before the moment of hesitation had given way to action a deed of Nature's own violence overwhelmed them both. A fierce shriek of the storm had been answered by a splitting crash over their heads, and ere they could leap aside a mass of falling beech tree had thundered down on them. Ulrich von Gradwitz found himself stretched on the ground, one arm numb beneath him and the other held almost as helplessly in a tight tangle of forked branches, while both legs were pinned beneath the fallen mass. His heavy shooting-boots had saved his feet from being crushed to pieces, but if his fractures were not as serious as they might have been, at least it was evident that he could not move from his present position till some one came to release him. The descending twig had slashed the skin of his face, and he had to wink away some drops of blood from his eyelashes before he could take in a general view of the disaster. At his side, so near that under ordinary circumstances he could almost have touched him, lay Georg Znaeym, alive and struggling, but obviously as helplessly pinioned down as himself. All round them lay a thick-strewn wreckage of splintered branches and broken twigs.

Relief at being alive and exasperation at his captive plight brought a strange medley of pious thank-offerings and sharp curses to Ulrich's lips. Georg, who was early blinded with the blood which trickled across his eyes, stopped his struggling for a moment to listen, and then gave a short, snarling laugh.

"So you're not killed, as you ought to be, but you're caught, anyway," he cried; "caught fast. Ho, what a jest, Ulrich von Gradwitz snared in his stolen forest. There's real justice for you!"

And he laughed again, mockingly and savagely.

"I'm caught in my own forest-land," retorted Ulrich. "When my men come to release us you will wish, perhaps, that you were in a better plight than caught poaching on a neighbour's land, shame on you."

Georg was silent for a moment; then he answered quietly:

"Are you sure that your men will find much to release? I have men, too, in the forest tonight, close behind me, and *they* will be here first and do the releasing. When they drag me out from under these damned branches it won't need much clumsiness on their part to roll this mass of trunk right over on the top of you. Your men will find you dead under a fallen beech tree. For form's sake I shall send my condolences to your family."

"It is a useful hint," said Ulrich fiercely. "My men had orders to follow in ten minutes time, seven of which must have gone by already, and when they get me out—I will remember the hint. Only as you will have met your death poaching on my lands I don't think I can decently send any message of condolence to your family."

"Good," snarled Georg, "good. We fight this quarrel out to the death, you and I and our foresters, with no cursed interlopers to come between us. Death and damnation to you, Ulrich von Gradwitz."

"The same to you, Georg Znaeym, forest-thief, game-snatcher."

Both men spoke with the bitterness of possible defeat before them, for each knew that it might be long before his men would seek him out or find him; it was a bare matter of chance which party would arrive first on the scene.

Both had now given up the useless struggle to free themselves from the mass of wood that held them down; Ulrich limited his endeavours to an effort to bring his one partially free arm near enough to his outer coat pocket to draw out his wine flask. Even when he had accomplished that operation it was long before he could manage the unscrewing of the stopper or get any of the liquid down his throat. But what a Heaven-sent draught it seemed! It was an open winter, and little snow had fallen as yet, hence the captives suffered less from the cold than might have been the case at that season of the year; nevertheless, the wine was warming and reviving to the wounded man, and he looked across with something like a throb of pity to where his enemy lay, just keeping the groans of pain and weariness from crossing his lips.

"Could you reach this flask if I threw it over to you?" asked Ulrich suddenly; "there is good wine in it, and one may as well be as comfortable as one can. Let us drink, even if tonight one of us dies."

"No, I can scarcely see anything; there is so much blood caked round my eyes," said Georg, "and in any case I don't drink wine with an enemy."

Ulrich was silent for a few minutes, and lay listening to the weary screeching of the wind. An idea was slowly forming and growing in his brain, an idea that gained strength every time that he looked across at the man who was fighting so grimly against pain and exhaustion. In the pain and languor that Ulrich himself was feeling the old fierce hatred seemed to be dying down.

"Neighbour," he said presently, "do as you please if your men come first. It was a fair compact. But as for me, I've changed my mind. If my men are the first to come you shall be the first to be helped, as though you were my guest. We have quarrelled like devils all our lives over this stupid strip of forest, where the trees can't even stand upright in a breath of wind. Lying here tonight thinking I've come to think we've been rather fools; there are better things in life than getting the better of a boundary dispute. Neighbour, if you will help me to bury the old quarrel I—I will ask you to be my friend."

Georg Znaeym was silent for so long that Ulrich thought, perhaps, he had fainted with the pain of his injuries. Then he spoke slowly and in jerks.

"How the whole region would stare and gabble if we rode into the market-square together. No one living can remember seeing a Znaeym and a von Gradwitz talking to one another in friendship. And what peace there would be among the forester folk if we ended our feud tonight. And if we choose to make peace among our people there is none other to interfere, no interlopers from outside . . . You would come and keep the Sylvester night beneath my roof, and I would come and feast on some high day at your castle . . . I would never fire a shot on your land, save when you invited me as a guest; and you should come and shoot with me down in the marshes where the wildfowl are. In all the countryside there are none that could hinder if we willed to make peace. I never thought to have wanted to do other than hate you all my life, but I think I have changed my mind about things too, this last half-hour. And you offered me your wineflask . . . Ulrich von Gradwitz, I will be your friend."

For a space both men were silent, turning over in their minds the wonderful changes that this dramatic reconciliation would bring about. In the cold, gloomy forest, with the wind tearing in fitful gusts through the naked branches and whistling round the tree-trunks, they lay and waited for the help that would now bring release and succour to both parties. And each prayed a private prayer that his men might be the first to arrive, so that he might be the first to show honourable attention to the enemy that had become a friend.

Presently, as the wind dropped for a moment, Ulrich broke silence.

"Let's shout for help," he said; he said; "in this lull our voices may carry a little way."

"They won't carry far through the trees and undergrowth," said Georg, "but we can try. Together, then."

The two raised their voices in a prolonged hunting call.

"Together again," said Ulrich a few minutes later, after listening in vain for an answering halloo.

"I heard nothing but the pestilential wind," said Georg hoarsely.

There was silence again for some minutes, and then Ulrich gave a joyful cry.

"I can see figures coming through the wood. They are following in the way I came down the hillside."

Both men raised their voices in as loud a shout as they could muster.

"They hear us! They've stopped. Now they see us. They're running down the hill towards us," cried Ulrich.

"How many of them are there?" asked Georg.

"I can't see distinctly," said Ulrich; "nine or ten,"

"Then they are yours," said Georg; "I had only seven out with me."

"They are making all the speed they can, brave lads," said Ulrich gladly.

"Are they your men?" asked Georg. "Are they your men?" he repeated impatiently as Ulrich did not answer.

"No," said Ulrich with a laugh, the idiotic chattering laugh of a man unstrung with hideous fear.

"Who are they?" asked Georg quickly, straining his eyes to see what the other would gladly not have seen.

"Wolves."

QUAIL SEED

"THE OUTLOOK is not encouraging for us smaller businesses," said Mr. Scarrick to the artist and his sister, who had taken rooms over his suburban grocery store. "These big concerns are offering all sorts of attractions to the shopping public which we couldn't afford to imitate, even on a small scale—reading-rooms and play-rooms and gramophones and Heaven knows what. People don't care to buy half a pound of sugar nowadays unless they can listen to Harry Lauder and have the latest Australian cricket scores ticked off before their eyes. With the big Christmas stock we've got in we ought to keep half a dozen assistants hard at work, but as it is my nephew Jimmy and myself can pretty well attend to it ourselves. It's a nice stock of goods, too, if I could only run it off in a few weeks time, but there's no chance of that—not unless the London line was to get snowed up for a fortnight before Christmas. I did have a sort of idea of engaging Miss Luffcombe to give recitations during afternoons; she made a great hit at the Post Office entertainment with her rendering of 'Little Beatrice's Resolve'."

"Anything less likely to make your shop a fashionable shopping centre I can't imagine," said the artist, with a very genuine shudder; "if I were trying to decide between the merits of Carlsbad plums and confected figs as a winter dessert it would infuriate me to have my train of thought entangled with little Beatrice's resolve to be an Angel of Light or a girl scout. No," he continued, "the desire to get something thrown in for nothing is a ruling passion with the feminine shopper, but you can't afford to pander effectively to it. Why not appeal to another instinct; which dominates not only the woman shopper but the male shopper—in fact, the entire human race?"

"What is that instinct, sir?" said the grocer.

*   *   *

Mrs. Greyes and Miss Fritten had missed the 2.18 to Town, and as there was not another train till 3.12 they thought that they might as well make their grocery purchases at Scarrick's. It would not be sensational, they agreed, but it would still be shopping.

For some minutes they had the shop almost to themselves, as far as customers were concerned, but while they were debating the respective virtues and blemishes of two competing brands of anchovy paste they were startled by an order, given across the counter, for six pomegranates and a packet of quail seed. Neither commodity was in general demand in that neighbourhood. Equally unusual was the style and appearance of the customer; about sixteen years old, with dark olive skin, large dusky eyes, and think, low-growing, blue-black hair, he might have made his living as an artist's model. As a matter of fact he did. The bowl of beaten brass that he produced for the reception of his purchases was distinctly the most astonishing variation on the string bag or marketing basket of suburban civilisation that his fellow-shoppers had ever seen. He threw a gold piece, apparently of some exotic currency, across the counter, and did not seem disposed to wait for any change that might be forthcoming.

"The wine and figs were not paid for yesterday," he said; "keep what is over of the money for our future purchases."

"A very strange-looking boy?" said Mrs. Greyes interrogatively to the grocer as soon as his customer had left.

"A foreigner, I believe," said Mr. Scarrick, with a shortness that was entirely out of keeping with his usually communicative manner.

"I wish for a pound and a half of the best coffee you have," said an authoritative voice a moment or two later. The speaker was a tall, authoritative-looking man of rather outlandish aspect, remarkable among other things for a full black beard, worn in a style more in vogue in early Assyria than in a London suburb of the present day.

"Has a dark-faced boy been here buying pomegranates?" he asked suddenly, as the coffee was being weighed out to him.

The two ladies almost jumped on hearing the grocer reply with an unblushing negative.

"We have a few pomegranates in stock," he continued, "but there has been no demand for them."

"My servant will fetch the coffee as usual," said the purchaser, producing a coin from a wonderful metal-work purse. As an apparent afterthought he fired out the question: "Have you, perhaps, any quail seed?"

"No," said the grocer, without hesitation, "we don't stock it."

"What will he deny next?" asked Mrs. Greyes under her breath. What made it seem so much worse was the fact that Mr. Scarrick had quite recently presided at a lecture on Savonarola.

Turning up the deep astrachan collar of his long coat, the stranger swept out of the shop, with the air, Miss Fritten afterwards described it, of a Satrap proroguing a Sanhedrim. Whether such a pleasant function ever fell to a Satrap's lot she was not quite certain, but the simile faithfully conveyed her meaning to a large circle of acquaintances.

"Don't let's bother about the 3.12," said Mrs. Greyes; "let's go and talk this over at Laura Lipping's. It's her day."

When the dark-faced boy arrived at the shop next day with his brass marketing bowl there was quite a fair gathering of customers, most of whom seemed to be spinning out their purchasing operations with the air of people who had very little to do with their time. In a voice that was heard all over the shop, perhaps because everybody was intently listening, he asked for a pound of honey and a packet of quail seed.

"More quail seed!" said Miss Fritten. "Those quails must be voracious, or else it isn't quail seed at all."

"I believe it's opium, and the bearded man is a detective," said Mrs. Greyes brilliantly.

"I don't," said Laura Lipping; "I'm sure it's something to do with the Portuguese Throne."

"More likely to be a Persian intrigue on behalf of the ex-Shah," said Miss Fritten; "the bearded man belongs to the Government Party. The quail-seed is a countersign, of course; Persia is almost next door to Palestine, and quails come into the Old Testament, you know."

"Only as a miracle," said her well-informed younger sister; "I've thought all along it was part of a love intrigue."

The boy who had so much interest and speculation centred on him was on the point of departing with his purchases when he was waylaid by

Jimmy, the nephew-apprentice, who, from his post at the cheese and bacon counter, commanded a good view of the street.

"We have some very fine Jaffa oranges," he said hurriedly, pointing to a corner where they were stored, behind a high rampart of biscuit tins. There was evidently more in the remark than met the ear. The boy flew at the oranges with the enthusiasm of a ferret finding a rabbit family at home after a long day of fruitless subterranean research. Almost at the same moment the bearded stranger stalked into the shop, and flung an order for a pound of dates and a tin of the best Smyrna halva across the counter. The most adventurous housewife in the locality had never heard of halva, but Mr. Scarrick was apparently able to produce the best Smyrna variety of it without a moment's hesitation.

"We might be living in the Arabian Nights," said Miss Fritten, excitedly.

"Hush! Listen," beseeched Mrs. Greyes.

"Has the dark-faced boy, of whom I spoke yesterday, been here today?" asked the stranger.

"We've had rather more people than usual in the shop today," said Mr. Scarrick, "but I can't recall a boy such as you describe."

Mrs. Greyes and Miss Fritten looked round triumphantly at their friends. It was, of course, deplorable that any one should treat the truth as an article temporarily and excusably out of stock, but they felt gratified that the vivid accounts they had given of Mr. Scarrick's traffic in falsehoods should receive confirmation at first hand.

"I shall never again be able to believe what he tells me about the absence of colouring matter in the jam," whispered an aunt of Mrs. Greyes tragically.

The mysterious stranger took his departure; Laura Lipping distinctly saw a snarl of baffled rage reveal itself behind his heavy moustache and upturned astrachan collar. After a cautious interval the seeker after oranges emerged from behind the biscuit tins, having apparently failed to find any individual orange that satisfied his requirements. He, too, took his departure, and the shop was slowly emptied of its parcel and gossip laden customers. It was Emily Yorling's "day", and most of the shoppers made their way to her drawing-room. To go direct from a shopping expedition to a tea party was what was known locally as "living in a whirl".

Two extra assistants had been engaged for the following afternoon, and their services were in brisk demand; the shop was crowded. People bought and bought, and never seemed to get to the end of their lists. Mr. Scarrick had never had so little difficulty in persuading customers to embark on new experiences in grocery wares. Even those women whose purchases were of modest proportions dawdled over them as though they had brutal, drunken husbands to go home to. The afternoon had dragged uneventfully on, and there was a distinct buzz of unpent excitement when a dark-eyed boy carrying a brass bowl entered the shop. The excitement seemed to have communicated itself to Mr. Scarrick; abruptly deserting a lady who was making insincere inquiries about the home life of the Bombay duck, he intercepted the newcomer on his way to the accustomed counter and informed him, amid a deathlike hush, that he had run out of quail seed.

The boy looked nervously round the shop, and turned hesitatingly to go. He was again intercepted, this time by the nephew, who darted out from behind his counter and said something about a better line of oranges. The boy's hesitation vanished; he almost scuttled into the obscurity of the orange corner. There was an expectant turn of public attention towards the door, and the tall, bearded stranger made a really effective entrance. The aunt of Mrs. Greyes declared afterwards that she found herself subconsciously repeating, "The Assyrian came down like a wolf on the fold" under her breath, and she was generally believed.

The newcomer, too, was stopped before he reached the counter, but not by Mr. Scarrick or his assistant. A heavily veiled lady, whom no one had hitherto noticed, rose languidly from a seat and greeted him in a clear, penetrating voice.

"Your Excellency does his shopping himself?" she said.

"I order the things myself," he explained; "I find it difficult to make my servants understand."

In a lower, but still perfectly audible, voice the veiled lady gave him a piece of casual information.

"They have some excellent Jaffa oranges here." Then with a tinkling laugh she passed out of the shop.

The man glared all round the shop, and then, fixing his eyes instinctively on the barrier of biscuit tins, demanded loudly of the grocer: "You have, perhaps, some good Jaffa oranges?"

Every one expected an instant denial on the part of Mr. Scarrick of any such possession. Before he could answer, however, the boy had broken forth from his sanctuary. Holding his empty brass bowl before him he passed out into the street. His face was variously described afterwards as masked with studied indifference, overspread with ghastly pallor, and blazing with defiance. Some said that his teeth chattered, others that he went out whistling the Persian National Hymn. There was no mistaking, however, the effect produced by the encounter on the man who had seemed to force it. If a rabid dog or a rattlesnake had suddenly thrust its companionship on him he could scarcely have displayed a greater access of terror. His air of authority and assertiveness had gone, his masterful stride had given way to a furtive pacing to and fro, as of an animal seeking an outlet for escape. In a dazed perfunctory manner, always with his eyes turning to watch the shop entrance, he gave a few random orders, which the grocer made a show of entering in his book. Now and then he walked out into the street, looked anxiously in all directions, and hurried back to keep up his pretence of shopping. From one of these sorties he did not return; he had dashed away into the dusk, and neither he nor the dark-faced boy nor the veiled lady were seen again by the expectant crowds that continued to throng the Scarrick establishment for days to come.

*   *   *

"I can never thank you and your sister sufficiently," said the grocer.

"We enjoyed the fun of it," said the artist modestly, "and as for the model, it was a welcome variation on posing for hours for 'The Lost Hylas'."

"At any rate," said the grocer, "I insist on paying for the hire of the black beard."

CANOSSA

DEMOSTHENES PLATTERBAFF, the eminent Unrest Inducer, stood on his trial for a serious offence, and the eyes of the political world were focussed on the jury. The offence, it should be stated, was serious for the Government rather than for the prisoner. He had blown up the Albert Hall on the eve of the great Liberal Federation Tango Tea, the occasion on which the Chancellor of the Exchequer was expected to propound his new theory: "Do partridges spread infectious diseases?" Platterbaff had chosen his time well; the Tango Tea had been hurriedly postponed, but there were other political fixtures which could not be put off under any circumstances. The day after the trial there was to be a by-election at Nemesis-on-Hand, and it had been openly announced in the division that if Platterbaff were languishing in gaol on polling day the Government candidate would be "outed" to a certainty. Unfortunately, there could be no doubt or misconception as to Platterbaff's guilt. He had not only pleaded guilty, but had expressed his intention of repeating his escapade in other directions as soon as circumstances permitted; throughout the trial he was busy examining a small model of the Free Trade Hall in Manchester. The jury could not possibly find that the prisoner had not deliberately and intentionally blown up the Albert Hall; the question was: Could they find any extenuating circumstances which would permit of an acquittal? Of course any sentence which the law might feel compelled to inflict would be followed by an immediate pardon, but it was highly desirable, from the Government's point of view, that the necessity for such an exercise of clemency should not arise. A headlong pardon, on the eve of a by-election, with threats of a heavy voting defection if it were withheld or even delayed, would not necessarily be a surrender, but it would look like one. Opponents would be only too ready to attribute ungenerous motives. Hence the anxiety in the crowded Court, and in the little groups gathered round the tape-machines in Whitehall and Downing Street and other affected centres.

The jury returned from considering their verdict; there was a flutter, an excited murmur, a deathlike hush. The foreman delivered his message:

"The jury find the prisoner guilty of blowing up the Albert Hall. The jury wish to add a rider drawing attention to the fact that a by-election is pending in the Parliamentary division of Nemesis-on-Hand."

"That, of course," said the Government Prosecutor, springing to his feet, "is equivalent to an acquittal?"

"I hardly think so," said the Judge, coldly; "I feel obliged to sentence the prisoner to a week's imprisonment."

"And may the Lord have mercy on the poll," a Junior Counsel exclaimed irreverently.

It was a scandalous sentence, but then the Judge was not on the Ministerial side in politics.

The verdict and sentence were made known to the public at twenty minutes past five in the afternoon; at half-past five a dense crowd was massed outside the Prime Minister's residence lustily singing, to the air of "Trelawney":

> *"And should our Hero rot in gaol,*
> *For e'en a single day,*
> *There's Fifteen Hundred Voting Men*
> *Will vote the other way."*

"Fifteen hundred," said the Prime Minister, with a shudder; "it's too horrible to think of. Our majority last time was only a thousand and seven."

"The poll opens at eight tomorrow morning," said the Chief Organiser; "we must have him out by 7 A.M."

"Seven-thirty," amended the Prime Minister; "we must avoid any appearance of precipitancy."

"Not later than seven-thirty, then," said the Chief Organiser; "I have promised the agent down there that he shall be able to display posters announcing 'Platterbaff is Out,' before the poll opens. He said it was our only chance of getting a telegram 'Radprop is In' tonight."

At half-past seven the next morning the Prime Minister and the

Chief Organiser sat at breakfast, making a perfunctory meal, and awaiting the return of the Home Secretary, who had gone in person to superintend the releasing of Platterbaff. Despite the earliness of the hour a small crowd had gathered in the street outside, and the horrible menacing Trelawney refrain of the "Fifteen Hundred Voting Men" came in a steady, monotonous chant.

"They will cheer presently when they hear the news," said the Prime Minister hopefully; "hark! They are booing some one now! That must be McKenna."

The Home Secretary entered the room a moment later, disaster written on his face.

"He won't go!" he exclaimed.

"Won't go? Won't leave gaol?"

"He won't go unless he has a brass band. He says he never has left prison without a brass band to play him out, and he's not going to go without one now."

"But surely that sort of thing is provided by his supporters and admirers?" said the Prime Minister; "we can hardly be supposed to supply a released prisoner with a brass band. How on earth could we defend it on the Estimates?"

"His supporters say it is up to us to provide the music," said the Home Secretary; "they say we put him in prison, and it's our affair to see that he leaves it in a respectable manner. Anyway, he won't go unless he has a band."

The telephone squealed shrilly; it was a trunk call from Nemesis.

"Poll opens in five minutes. Is Platterbaff out yet? In Heaven's name, why—"

The Chief Organiser rang off.

"This is not a moment for standing on dignity," he observed bluntly; "musicians must be supplied at once. Platterbaff must have his band."

"Where are you going to find the musicians?" asked the Home Secretary wearily; "we can't employ a military band, in fact, I don't think he'd have one if we offered it, and there ain't any others. There's a musicians' strike on, I suppose you know."

"Can't you get a strike permit?" asked the Organiser.

"I'll try," said the Home Secretary, and went to the telephone.

Eight o'clock struck. The crowd outside chanted with an increasing volume of sound:

"Will vote the other way."

A telegram was brought in. It was from the central committee rooms at Nemesis. "Losing twenty votes per minute," was its brief message.

Ten o'clock struck. The Prime Minister, the Home Secretary, the Chief Organiser, and several earnest helpful friends were gathered in the inner gateway of the prison, talking volubly to Demosthenes Platterbaff, who stood with folded arms and squarely planted feet, silent in their midst. Golden-tongued legislators whose eloquence had swayed the Marconi Inquiry Committee, or at any rate the greater part of it, expended their arts of oratory in vain on this stubborn unyielding man. Without a band he would not go; and they had no band.

A quarter past ten, half-past. A constant stream of telegraph boys poured in through the prison gates.

"Yamley's factory hands just voted you can guess how," ran a despairing message, and the others were all of the same tenour. Nemesis was going the way of Reading.

"Have you any band instruments of an easy nature to play?" demanded the Chief Organiser of the Prison Governor; "drums, cymbals, those sort of things?"

"The warders have a private band of their own," said the Governor, "but of course I couldn't allow the men themselves—"

"Lend us the instruments," said the Chief Organiser.

One of the earnest helpful friends was a skilled performer on the cornet, the Cabinet Ministers were able to clash cymbals more or less in tune, and the Chief Organiser has some knowledge of the drum.

"What tune would you prefer?" he asked Platterbaff.

"The popular song of the moment," replied the Agitator after a moment's reflection.

It was a tune they had all heard hundreds of times, so there was no difficulty in turning out a passable imitation of it. To the improvised strains of "I didn't want to do it" the prisoner strode forth to freedom. The word of the song had reference, it was understood, to the incarcerating Government and not to the destroyer of the Albert Hall.

The seat was lost, after all, by a narrow majority. The local Trade Unionists took offence at the fact of Cabinet Ministers having personally acted as strike-breakers, and even the release of Platterbaff failed to pacify them.

The seat was lost, but Ministers had scored a moral victory. They had shown that they knew when and how to yield.

THE THREAT

SIR LULWORTH Quayne sat in the lounge of his favourite restaurant, the Gallus Bankiva, discussing the weaknesses of the world with his nephew, who had lately returned from a much-enlivened exile in the wilds of Mexico. It was that blessed season of the year when the asparagus and the plover's egg are abroad in the land, and the oyster has not yet withdrawn into it's summer entrenchments, and Sir Lulworth and his nephew were in that enlightened after-dinner mood when politics are seen in their right perspective, even the politics of Mexico.

"Most of the revolutions that take place in this country nowadays," said Sir Lulworth, "are the product of moments of legislative panic. Take, for instance, one of the most dramatic reforms that has been carried through Parliament in the lifetime of this generation. It happened shortly after the coal strike, of unblessed memory. To you, who have been plunged up to the neck in events of a more tangled and tumbled description, the things I am going to tell you of may seem of secondary interest, but after all we had to live in the midst of them."

Sir Lulworth interrupted himself for a moment to say a few kind words to the liqueur brandy he had just tasted, and them resumed his narrative.

"Whether one sympathises with the agitation for female suffrage or not one has to admit that its promoters showed tireless energy and considerable enterprise in devising and putting into action new methods for accomplishing their ends. As a rule they were a nuisance and a weariness to the flesh, but there were times when they verged on the picturesque. There was the famous occasion when they enlivened and diversified the customary pageantry of the Royal progress to open Parliament by letting loose thousands of parrots, which had been carefully trained to scream 'Votes for women,' and which circled round his Majesty's coach in a clamorous cloud of green, and grey and scarlet. It was really rather a striking episode from the spectacular point of view; unfortunately, however, for its devisers, the secret of their intentions had not been well kept, and their opponents let loose at the same moment a rival swarm of parrots, which screeched 'I *don't* think' and other hostile cries, thereby robbing the demonstration of the unanimity which alone could have made it politically impressive. In the process of recapture the birds learned a quantity of additional language which unfitted them for further service in the Suffragette cause; some of the green ones were secured by ardent Home Rule propagandists and trained to disturb the serenity of Orange meetings by pessimistic reflections on Sir Edward Carson's destination in the life to come. In fact, the bird in politics is a factor that seems to have come to stay; quite recently, at a political gathering held in a dimly-lighted place of worship, the congregation gave a respectful hearing for nearly ten minutes to a jackdaw from Wapping, under the impression that they were listening to the Chancellor of the Exchequer, who was late in arriving."

"But the Suffragettes," interrupted the nephew; "what did they do next?"

"After the bird fiasco," said Sir Lulworth, "the militant section made a demonstration of a more aggressive nature; they assembled in force on the opening day of the Royal Academy Exhibition and destroyed some three or four hundred of the pictures. This proved an even worse failure than the parrot business; every one agreed that there was always far too many pictures in the Academy Exhibition, and the drastic weeding out of a few hundred canvases was regarded as a positive improvement. Moreover, from the artists' point of view it was realised that the outrage constituted a sort of compensation for those whose works were persistently 'skied', since out of sight meant also out of reach. Altogether it was one of the most successful and popular exhibitions that the Academy had held for many years. Then the fair agitators fell back on some of their earlier methods; they wrote sweetly argumentative plays to prove that they ought to have the vote, they smashed windows to show that they must have the vote, and they kicked Cabinet Ministers to demonstrate that they'd better have the vote, and still the coldly reasoned or unreasoned reply was that they'd better not. Their plight might have been summed up in a perversion of Gilbert's lines—

"Twenty voteless millions we,
    Voteless all against our will,
  Twenty years hence we shall be
    Twenty voteless millions still."

And of course the great idea for their master-stroke of strategy came from a masculine source. Lena Dubarri, who was the captain-general of their thinking department, met Waldo Orpington in the Mall one afternoon, just at a time when the fortunes of the Cause were at their lowest ebb. Waldo Orpington is a frivolous little fool who chirrups at drawing-room concerts and can recognise bits from different composers without referring to the programme, but all the same he occasionally has ideas. He didn't care a twopenny fiddlestring about the Cause, but he rather enjoyed the idea of having his finger in the political pie. Also it is possible, though I should think highly improbable, that he admired Lena Dubarri. Anyhow, when Lena gave a rather gloomy account of the existing state of things in the Suffragette World, Waldo was not merely sympathetic but ready with a practical suggestion. Turning his gaze westward along the Mall, towards the setting sun and Buckingham Palace, he was silent for a moment, and then said significantly, 'You have expended your energies and enterprise on labours of destruction; why has it never occurred to you to attempt something far more terrific?'

" 'What do you mean?' she asked him eagerly.

" 'Create.'

" 'Do you mean create disturbances? We've been doing nothing else for months,' she said.

"Waldo shook his head, and continued to look westward along the Mall. He's rather good at acting in an amateur sort of fashion. Lena followed his gaze, and then turned to him with a puzzled look of inquiry.

" 'Exactly,' said Waldo, in answer to her look.

" 'But—how can we create?' she asked; 'it's been done already.'

" 'Do it *again*,' said Waldo, 'and again and again—'

"Before he could finish the sentence she had kissed him. She declared afterwards that he was the first man she had ever kissed, and he declared that she was the first woman who had ever kissed him in the Mall, so they both secured a record of a kind.

"Within the next day or two a new departure was noticeable in Suffragette tactics. They gave up worrying Ministers and Parliament and took to worrying their own sympathisers and supporters—for funds. The ballot-box was temporarily forgotten in the cult of the collecting-box. The daughters of the horseleech were not more persistent in their demands, the financiers of the tottering ancien regime were not more desperate in their expedients for raising money than the Suffragist workers of all sections at this juncture, and in one way and another, by fair means and normal, they really got together a very useful sum. What they were going to do with it no one seemed to know, not even those who were most active in collecting work. The secret on this occasion had been well kept. Certain transactions that leaked out from time to time only added to the mystery of the situation.

" 'Don't you long to know what we are going to do with our treasure hoard?' Lena asked the Prime Minister one day when she happened to sit next to him at a whist drive at the Chinese Embassy.

" 'I was hoping you were going to try a little personal bribery,' he responded banteringly, but some genuine anxiety and curiosity lay behind the lightness of his chaff; 'of course I know,' he added, 'that you have been buying up building sites in commanding situations in and around the Metropolis. Two or three, I'm told, are on the road to Brighton, and another near Ascot. You don't mean to fortify them, do you?'

" 'Something more insidious than that,' she said; 'you could prevent us from building forts; you can't prevent us from erecting an exact replica of the Victoria Memorial on each of those sites. They're all private property, with no building restrictions attached.'

"'Which memorial?' he asked; 'not the one in front of Buckingham Palace? Surely not that one?'

" 'That one,' she said.

" 'My dear lady,' he cried, 'you can't be serious. It is a beautiful and imposing work of art—at any rate one is getting accustomed to it, and even if one doesn't happen to admire it one can always look in another direction. But imagine what life would be like if one saw that erection confronting one wherever one went. Imagine the effect on people with tired, harassed nerves who saw it three times on the way to Brighton and three times on the way back. Imagine seeing it dominate the landscape at Ascot, and trying to keep your eye off it on the Sandwich golf links. What have your countrymen done to deserve such a thing?'

" 'They have refused us the vote,' said Lena bitterly.

"The Prime Minister always declared himself an opponent of anything savouring of panic legislation, but he brought a Bill into Parliament forthwith and successfully appealed to both Houses to pass it through all its stages within the week. And that is how we got one of the most glorious measures of the century."

"A measure conferring the vote on women?" asked the nephew.

"Oh dear, no. An Act which made it a penal offence to erect commemorative statuary anywhere within three miles of a public highway."

EXCEPTING MRS. PENTHERBY

IT WAS Reggie Bruttle's own idea for converting what had threatened to be an albino elephant into a beast of burden that should help him along the stony road of his finances. "The Limes," which had come to him by inheritance without any accompanying provision for its upkeep, was one of those pretentious, unaccommodating mansions which none but a man of wealth could afford to live in, and which not one wealthy man in a hundred would choose on its merits. It might easily languish in the estate market for years, set round with noticeboards proclaiming it, in the eyes of a sceptical world, to be an eminently desirable residence.

Reggie's scheme was to turn it into the headquarters of a prolonged country-house party, in session during the months from October till the end of March—a party consisting of young or youngish people of both sexes, too poor to be able to do much hunting or shooting on a serious scale, but keen on getting their fill of golf, bridge, dancing, and occasional theatre-going. No one was to be on the footing of a paying guest, but every one was to rank as a paying host; a committee would look after the catering and expenditure, and an informal subcommittee would make itself useful in helping forward the amusement side of the scheme.

As it was only an experiment, there was to be a general agreement on the part of those involved in it to be as lenient and mutually helpful to one another as possible. Already a promising nucleus, including one or two young married couples, had been got together, and the thing seemed to be fairly launched.

"With good management and a little unobtrusive hard work, I think the thing ought to be a success," said Reggie, and Reggie was one of those people who are painstaking first and optimistic afterwards.

"There is one rock on which you will unfailingly come to grief, manage you never so wisely," said Major Dagberry, cheerfully; "the women will quarrel. Mind you," continued this prophet of disaster, "I don't say that some of the men won't quarrel too, probably they will; but the women are bound to. You can't prevent it; it's in the nature of the sex. The hand that rocks the cradle rocks the world, in a volcanic sense. A woman will endure discomforts, and make sacrifices, and go without things to an heroic extent, but the one luxury she will not go without is her quarrels. No matter where she may be, or how transient her appearance on a scene, she will instal her feminine feuds as assuredly as a Frenchman would concoct soup in the waste of the Arctic regions. At the commencement of a sea voyage, before the male traveller knows half a dozen of his fellow passengers by sight, the average woman will have started a couple of enmities, and laid in material for one or two more—provided, of course, that there are sufficient women aboard to permit quarrelling in the plural. If there's no one else she will quarrel with the stewardess. This experiment of yours is to run for six months; in less than five weeks there will be war to the knife declaring itself in half a dozen different directions."

"Oh, come, there are only eight women in the party; they won't pick quarrels quite so soon as that," protested Reggie.

"They won't all originate quarrels, perhaps," conceded the Major, "but they will all take sides, and just as Christmas is upon you, with its conventions of peace and good will, you will find yourself in for a glacial epoch of cold, unforgiving hostility, with an occasional Etna flare of open warfare. You can't help it, old boy; but, at any rate, you can't say you were not warned."

The first five weeks of the venture falsified Major Dagberry's prediction and justified Reggie's optimism. There were, of course, occasional small bickerings, and the existence of certain jealousies might be detected below the surface of everyday intercourse; but, on the whole, the womenfolk got on remarkably well together. There was, however, a notable exception. It had not taken five weeks for Mrs. Pentherby to get herself cordially disliked by the members of her own sex; five days had been amply sufficient. Most of the women declared that they had detested her the moment they set eyes on her; but that was probably an afterthought.

With the menfolk she got on well enough, without being of the type of woman who can only bask in male society; neither was she lacking in the general qualities which make an individual useful and desirable as a member of a cooperative community. She did not try to "get the better of" her fellow-hosts by snatching little advantages or cleverly evading her just contributions; she was not inclined to be boring or snobbish in the way of personal reminiscence. She played a fair game of bridge, and her card-room manners were irreproachable. But wherever she came in contact with her own sex the light of battle kindled at once; her talent of arousing animosity seemed to border on positive genius.

Whether the object of her attentions was thick-skinned or sensitive, quick-tempered or good-natured, Mrs. Pentherby managed to achieve the same effect. She exposed little weaknesses, she prodded sore places, she snubbed enthusiasms, she was generally right in a matter of argument, or, if wrong, she somehow contrived to make her adversary appear foolish and opinionated. She did, and said, horrible things in a matter-of-fact innocent way, and she did, and said, matter-of-fact innocent things in a horrible way. In short, the unanimous feminine verdict on her was that she was objectionable.

There was no question of taking sides, as the Major had anticipated; in fact, dislike of Mrs. Pentherby was almost a bond of union between the other women, and more than one threatening disagreement had been rapidly dissipated by her obvious and malicious attempts to inflame and extend it; and the most irritating thing about her was her successful assumption of unruffled composure at moments when the tempers of her adversaries were with difficulty kept under control. She made her most scathing remarks in the tone of a tube conductor announcing that the next station is Brompton Road—the measured, listless tone of one who knows he is right, but is utterly indifferent to the fact that he proclaims.

On one occasion Mrs. Val Gwepton, who was not blessed with the most reposeful of temperaments, fairly let herself go, and gave Mrs. Pentherby a vivid and truthful resume of her opinion of her. The object of this unpent storm of accumulated animosity waited patiently for a lull, and then remarked quietly to the angry little woman—

"And now, my dear Mrs. Gwepton, let me tell you something that I've been wanting to say for the last two or three minutes, only you wouldn't given me a chance; you've got a hairpin dropping out on the left side. You thin-haired women always find it difficult to keep your hairpins in."

"What can one do with a woman like that?" Mrs. Val demanded afterwards of a sympathising audience.

Of course, Reggie received numerous hints as to the unpopularity of this jarring personality. His sister-in-law openly tackled him on the subject of her many enormities. Reggie listened with the attenuated regret that one bestows on an earthquake disaster in Bolivia or a crop failure in Eastern Turkestan, events which seem so distant that one can almost persuade oneself they haven't happened.

"That woman has got some hold over him," opined his sister-in-law, darkly; "either she is helping him to finance the show, and presumes on the fact, or else, which Heaven forbid, he's got some queer infatuation for her. Men do take the most extraordinary fancies."

Matters never came exactly to a crisis. Mrs. Pentherby, as a source of personal offence, spread herself over so wide an area that no one woman of the party felt impelled to rise up and declare that she absolutely refused to stay another week in the same house with her. What is everybody's tragedy is nobody's tragedy. There was ever a certain consolation in comparing notes as to specific acts of offence. Reggie's sister-in-law had the added interest of trying to discover the secret bond which blunted his condemnation of Mrs. Pentherby's long catalogue of misdeeds. There was little to go on from his manner towards her in public, but he remained obstinately unimpressed by anything that was said against her in private.

With the one exception of Mrs. Pentherby's unpopularity, the house-party scheme was a success on its first trial, and there was no difficulty about reconstructing it on the same lines for another winter session. It so happened that most of the women of the party, and two or three of the men, would not be available on this occasion, but Reggie had laid his plans well ahead and booked plenty of "fresh blood" for the departure. It would be, if any thing, rather a larger party than before.

"I'm so sorry I can't join this winter," said Reggie's sister-in-law, "but we must go to our cousins in Ireland; we've put them off so often.

What a shame! You'll have none of the same women this time."

"Excepting Mrs. Pentherby," said Reggie, demurely.

"Mrs. Pentherby! *Surely*, Reggie, you're not going to be so idiotic as to have that woman again! She'll set all the women's backs up just as she did this time. What *is* this mysterious hold she's go over you?"

"She's invaluable," said Reggie; "she's my official quarreller."

"Your—what did you say?" gasped his sister-in-law.

"I introduced her into the house-party for the express purpose of concentrating the feuds and quarrelling that would otherwise have broken out in all directions among the womenkind. I didn't need the advice and warning of sundry friends to foresee that we shouldn't get through six months of close companionship without a certain amount of pecking and sparring, so I thought the best thing was to localise and sterilise it in one process. Of course, I made it well worth the lady's while, and as she didn't know any of you from Adam, and you don't even know her real name, she didn't mind getting herself disliked in a useful cause."

"You mean to say she was in the know all the time?"

"Of course she was, and so were one or two of the men, so she was able to have a good laugh with us behind the scenes when she'd done anything particularly outrageous. And she really enjoyed herself. You see, she's in the position of poor relation in a rather pugnacious family, and her life has been largely spent in smoothing over other people's quarrels. You can imagine the welcome relief of being able to go about saying and doing perfectly exasperating things to a whole houseful of women—and all in the cause of peace."

"I think you are the most odious person in the whole world," said Reggie's sister-in-law. Which was not strictly true; more than anybody, more than ever she disliked Mrs. Pentherby. It was impossible to calculate how many quarrels that woman had done her out of.

MARK

AUGUSTUS MELLOWKENT was a novelist with a future; that is to say, a limited but increasing number of people read his books, and there seemed good reason to suppose that if he steadily continued to turn out novels year by year a progressively increasing circle of readers would acquire the Mellowkent habit, and demand his works from the libraries and bookstalls. At the instigation of his publisher he had discarded the baptismal Augustus and taken the front name of Mark.

"Women like a name that suggests some one strong and silent, able but unwilling to answer questions. Augustus merely suggests idle splendour, but such a name as Mark Mellowkent, besides being alliterative, conjures up a vision of some one strong and beautiful and good, a sort of blend of Georges Carpentier and the Reverend What's-his-name."

One morning in December Augustus sat in his writing-room, at work on the third chapter of his eighth novel. He had described at some length, for the benefit of those who could not imagine it, what a rectory garden looks like in July; he was now engaged in describing at greater length the feelings of a young girl, daughter of a long line of rectors and archdeacons, when she discovers for the first time that the postman is attractive.

Their eyes met, for a brief moment, as he handed her two circulars and the fat wrapper-bound bulk of the East Essex News. Their eyes met, for the merest fraction of a second, yet nothing could ever be quite the same again. Cost what it might she felt that she must speak, must break the intolerable, unreal silence that had fallen on them. "How is your mother's rheumatism?" she said.

The author's labours were cut short by the sudden intrusion of a maidservant.

"A gentleman to see you, sir," said the maid, handing a card with the name Caiaphas Dwelf inscribed on it; "says it's important."

Mellowkent hesitated and yielded; the importance of the visitor's mission was probably illusory, but he had never met any one with the name Caiaphas before. It would be at least a new experience.

Mr. Dwelf was a man of indefinite age; his high, narrow forehead, cold grey eyes, and determined manner bespoke an unflinching purpose. He had a large book under his arm, and there seemed every probability that he had left a package of similar volumes in the hall. He took a seat before it had been offered him, placed the book on the table, and began to address Mellowkent in the manner of an "open letter."

"You are a literary man, the author of several well-known books—"

"I am engage on a book at the present moment—rather busily engaged," said Mellowkent, pointedly.

"Exactly," said the intruder; "time with you is a commodity of considerable importance. Minutes, even, have their value."

"They have," agreed Mellowkent, looking at his watch.

"That," said Caiaphas, "is why this book that I am introducing to your notice is not a book that you can afford to be without. *Right Here* is indispensable for the writing man; it is no ordinary encyclopedia, or I should not trouble to show it to you. It is an inexhaustible mine of concise information—"

"On a shelf at my elbow," said the author, "I have a row of reference books that supply me with all the information I am likely to require."

"Here," persisted the would-be salesman, "you have it all in one compact volume. No matter what the subject may be which you wish to look up, or the fact you desire to verify, *Right Here* gives you all that you want to know in the briefest and most enlightening form. Historical reference, for instance; career of John Huss, let us say. Here we are: 'Huss, John, celebrated religious reformer. Born 1369, burned at Constance 1415. The Emperor Sigismund universally blamed.'"

"If he had been burnt in these days every one would have suspected the Suffragettes," observed Mellowkent.

"Poultry-keeping, now," resumed Caiaphas, "that's a subject that might crop up in a novel dealing with English country life. Here we have all about it: 'The Leghorn as egg-producer. Lack of maternal instinct in the Minorca. Gapes in chickens, its cause and cure. Ducklings for the early market, how fattened.' There, you see, there it all is, nothing lacking."

"Except the maternal instinct in the Minorca, and that you could hardly be expected to supply."

"Sporting records, that's important, too; now how many men, sporting men even, are there who can say off-hand what horse won the Derby in any particular year? Now it's just a little thing of that sort—"

"My dear sir," interrupted Mellowkent, "there are at least four men in my club who can not only tell me what horse won in any given year, but what horse ought to have won and why it didn't. If your book could supply a method for protecting one from information of that sort it would do more than anything you have yet claimed for it."

"Geography," said Caiaphas, imperturbably; "that's a thing that a busy man, writing at high pressure, may easily make a slip over. Only the other day a well-known author made the Volga flow into the Black Sea instead of the Caspian; now, with this book—"

"On a polished rose-wood stand behind you there reposes a reliable and up-to-date atlas," said Mellowkent; "and now I must really ask you to be going."

"An atlas," said Caiaphas, "gives merely the chart of the river's course, and indicates the principal towns that it passes. Now Right Here gives you the scenery, traffic, ferry-boat charges, the prevalent types of fish, boatmen's slang terms, and hours of sailing of the principal river steamers. If gives you—"

Mellowkent sat and watched the hard-featured, resolute, pitiless salesman, as he sat doggedly in the chair wherein he had installed himself, unflinchingly extolling the merits of his undesired wares. A spirit of wistful emulation took possession of the author; why could he not live up to the cold stern name he had adopted? Why must he sit here weakly and listen to this weary, unconvincing tirade, why could he not be Mark Mellowkent for a few brief moments, and meet this man on level terms?

A sudden inspiration flashed across his.

"Have you read my last book, *The Cageless Linnet*?" he asked.

"I don't read novels," said Caiaphas tersely.

"Oh, but you ought to read this one, every one ought to," exclaimed Mellowkent, fishing the book down from a shelf; "published at six shillings, you can have it at four-and-six. There is a bit in chapter five that I feel sure you would like, where Emma is alone in the birch copse waiting for Harold Huntingdon—that is the man her family want her to marry. She really wants to marry him, too, but she does not discover that till chapter fifteen. Listen: 'Far as the eye could stretch rolled the mauve and purple billows of heather, lit up here and there with the glowing yellow of gorse and broom, and edged round with the delicate greys and silver and green of the young birch trees. Tiny blue and brown butterflies fluttered above the fronds of heather, revelling in the sunlight, and overhead the larks were singing as only larks can sing. It was a day when all Nature—' "

"In *Right Here* you have full information on all branches of Nature study," broke in the bookagent, with a tired note sounding in his voice for the first time; "forestry, insect life, bird migration, reclamation of waste lands. As I was saying, no man who has to deal with the varied interests of life—"

"I wonder if you would care for one of my earlier books, *The Reluctance of Lady Cullumpton*," said Mellowkent, hunting again through the bookshelf; "some people consider it my best novel. Ah, here it is. I see there are one or two spots on the cover, so I won't ask more than three-and-ninepence for it. Do let me read you how it opens:

"'Beatrice Lady Cullumpton entered the long, dimly-lit drawing-room, her eyes blazing with a hope that she guessed to be groundless, her lips trembling with a fear that she could not disguise. In her hand she carried a small fan, a fragile toy of lace and satinwood. Something snapped as she entered the room; she had crushed the fan into a dozen pieces.'

"There, what do you think of that for an opening? It tells you at once that there's something afoot."

"I don't read novels," said Caiaphas sullenly.

"But just think what a resource they are," exclaimed the author, "on long winter evenings, or perhaps when you are laid up with a strained ankle—a thing that might happen to any one; or if you were staying in a house-party with persistent wet weather and a stupid hostess and insufferably dull fellow-guests, you would just make an excuse that you had letters to write, go to your room, light a cigarette, and for three-and-ninepence you could plunge into the society of Beatrice Lady Cullumpton and her set. No one ought to travel without one or two of my novels in their luggage as a stand-by. A friend of mine said only the other day that he would as soon think of going into the tropics without quinine as of going on a visit without a couple of Mark Mellowkents in his kit-bag. Perhaps sensation is more in your line. I wonder if I've got a copy of *The Python's Kiss.*"

Caiaphas did not wait to be tempted with selections from that thrilling work of fiction. With a muttered remark about having no time to waste on monkey-talk, he gathered up his slighted volume and departed. He made no audible reply to Mellowkent's cheerful "Good morning," but the latter fancied that a look of respectful hatred flickered in the cold grey eyes.

THE HEDGEHOG

A "MIXED DOUBLE" of young people were contesting a game of lawn tennis at the Rectory garden party; for the past five-and-twenty years at least mixed doubles of young people had done exactly the same thing on exactly the same spot at about the same time of year. The young people changed and made way for others in the course of time, but very little else seemed to alter. The present players were sufficiently conscious of the social nature of the occasion to be concerned about their clothes and appearance, and sufficiently sport-loving to be keen on the game. Both their efforts and their appearance came under the fourfold scrutiny of a quartet of ladies sitting as official spectators on a bench immediately commanding the court. It was one of the accepted conditions of the Rectory garden party that four ladies, who usually knew very little about tennis and a great deal about the players, should sit at that particular spot and watch the game. It had also come to be almost a tradition that two ladies should be amiable, and that the other two should be Mrs. Dole and Mrs. Hatch-Mallard.

"What a singularly unbecoming way Eva Jonelet has taken to doing her hair in," said Mrs. Hatch-Mallard; "it's ugly hair at the best of times, but she needn't make it look ridiculous as well. Some one ought to tell her."

Eva Jonelet's hair might have escaped Mrs. Hatch-Mallard's condemnation if she could have forgotten the more glaring fact that Eva was Mrs. Dole's favourite niece. It would, perhaps, have been a more comfortable arrangement if Mrs. Hatch-Mallard and Mrs. Dole could have been asked to the Rectory on separate occasions, but there was only one garden party in the course of the year, and neither lady could have been omitted from the list of invitations without hopelessly wrecking the social peace of the parish.

"How pretty the yew trees look at this time of year," interposed a lady with a soft, silvery voice that suggested a chinchilla muff painted by Whistler.

"What do you mean by this time of year?" demanded Mrs. Hatch-Mallard. "Yew trees look beautiful at all times of the year. That is their great charm."

"Yew trees never look anything but hideous under any circumstances or at any time of year," said Mrs. Dole, with the slow, emphatic relish of one who contradicts for the pleasure of the thing. "They are only fit for graveyards and cemeteries."

Mrs. Hatch-Mallard gave a sardonic snort, which, being translated, meant that there were some people who were better fitted for cemeteries than for garden parties.

"What is the score, please?" asked the lady with the chinchilla voice.

The desired information was given her by a young gentleman in spotless white flannels, whose general toilet effect suggested solicitude rather than anxiety.

"What an odious young cub Bertie Dykson has become!" pronounced Mrs. Dole, remembering suddenly that Bertie was a favourite with Mrs. Hatch-Mallard. "The young men of today are not what they used to be twenty years ago."

"Of course not," said Mrs. Hatch-Mallard; "twenty years ago Bertie Dykson was just two years old, and you must expect some difference in appearance and manner and conversation between those two periods."

"Do you know," said Mrs. Dole, confidentially, "I shouldn't be surprised if that was intended to be clever."

"Have you any one interesting coming to stay with you, Mrs. Norbury?" asked the chinchilla voice, hastily; "you generally have a house party at this time of year."

"I've got a most interesting woman coming," said Mrs. Norbury, who had been mutely struggling for some chance to turn the conversation into a safe channel; "an old acquaintance of mine, Ada Bleek—"

"What an ugly name," said Mrs. Hatch-Mallard.

"She's descended from the de la Bliques, an old Huguenot family of Touraine, you know."

"There weren't any Huguenots in Touraine," said Mrs. Hatch-Mallard, who thought she might safely dispute any fact that was three hundred years old.

"Well, anyhow, she's coming to stay with me," continued Mrs. Norbury, bringing her story quickly down to the present day, "she arrives this evening, and she's highly clairvoyante, a seventh daughter of a seventh daughter, you now, and all that sort of thing."

"How very interesting," said the chinchilla voice; "Exwood is just the right place for her to come to, isn't it? There are supposed to be several ghosts there."

"That is why she was so anxious to come," said Mrs. Norbury; "she put off another engagement in order to accept my invitation. She's had visions and dreams, and all those sort of things, that have come true in a most marvellous manner, but she's never actually seen a ghost, and she's longing to have that experience. She belongs to that Research Society, you know."

"I expect she'll see the unhappy Lady Cullumpton, the most famous of all the Exwood ghosts," said Mrs. Dole; "my ancestor, you know, Sir Gervase Cullumpton, murdered his young bride in a fit of jealousy while they were on a visit to Exwood. He strangled her in the stables with a stirrup leather, just after they had come in from riding, and she is seen sometimes at dusk going about the lawns and the stable yard, in a long green habit, moaning and trying to get the thong from round her throat. I shall be most interested to hear if your friend sees—"

"I don't know why she should be expected to see a trashy, traditional apparition like the so-called Cullumpton ghost, that is only vouched for by housemaids and tipsy stableboys, when my uncle, who was the owner of Exwood, committed suicide there under the most tragical circumstances, and most certainly haunts the place."

"Mrs. Hatch-Mallard has evidently never read Popple's County History," said Mrs. Dole icily, "or she would know that the Cullumpton ghost has a wealth of evidence behind it—"

"Oh, Popple!" exclaimed Mrs. Hatch-Mallard scornfully; "any rubbishy old story is good enough for him. Popple, indeed! Now my uncle's ghost was seen by a Rural Dean, who was also a Justice of the Peace. I should think that would be good enough testimony for any one. Mrs.

Norbury, I shall take it as a deliberate personal affront if your clairvoyante friend sees any other ghost except that of my uncle."

"I daresay she won't see anything at all; she never has yet, you know," said Mrs. Norbury hopefully.

"It was a most unfortunate topic for me to have broached," she lamented afterwards to the owner of the chinchilla voice; "Exwood belongs to Mrs. Hatch-Mallard, and we've only got it on a short lease. A nephew of hers has been wanting to live there for some time, and if we offend her in any way she'll refuse to renew the lease. I sometimes think these garden-parties are a mistake."

The Norburys played bridge for the next three nights till nearly one o'clock; they did not care for the game, but it reduced the time at their guest's disposal for undesirable ghostly visitations.

"Miss Bleek is not likely to be in a frame of mind to see ghosts," said Hugo Norbury, "if she goes to bed with her brain awhirl with royal spades and no trumps and grand slams."

"I've talked to her for hours about Mrs. Hatch-Mallard's uncle," said his wife, "and pointed out the exact spot where he killed himself, and invented all sorts of impressive details, and I've found an old portrait of Lord John Russell and put it in her room, and told her that it's supposed to be a picture of the uncle in middle age. If Ada does see a ghost at all it certainly ought to be old Hatch-Mallard's. At any rate, we've done our best."

The precautions were in vain. On the third morning of her stay Ada Bleek came down late to breakfast, her eyes looking very tired, but ablaze with excitement, her hair done anyhow, and a large brown volume hugged under her arm.

"At last I've seen something supernatural!" she exclaimed, and gave Mrs. Norbury a fervent kiss, as though in gratitude for the opportunity afforded her.

"A ghost!" cried Mrs. Norbury, "not really!"

"Really and unmistakably!"

"Was it an oldish man in the dress of about fifty years ago?" asked Mrs. Norbury hopefully.

"Nothing of the sort," said Ada; "it was a white hedgehog."

"A white hedgehog!" exclaimed both the Norburys, in tones of disconcerted astonishment.

"A huge white hedgehog with baleful yellow eyes," said Ada; "I was lying half asleep in bed when suddenly I felt a sensation as of something sinister and unaccountable passing through the room. I sat up and looked round, and there, under the window, I saw an evil, creeping thing, a sort of monstrous hedgehog, of a dirty white colour, with black, loathsome claws that clicked and scraped along the floor, and narrow, yellow eyes of indescribable evil. It slithered along for a yard or two, always looking at me with its cruel, hideous eyes, then, when it reached the second window, which was open it clambered up the sill and vanished. I got up at once and went to the window; there wasn't a sign of it anywhere. Of course, I knew it must be something from another world, but it was not till I turned up Popple's chapter on local traditions that I realised what I had seen."

She turned eagerly to the large brown volume and read: " 'Nicholas Herison, an old miser, was hung at Batchford in 1763 for the murder of a farm lad who had accidentally discovered his secret hoard. His ghost is supposed to traverse the countryside, appearing sometimes as a white owl, sometimes as a huge white hedgehog.' "

"I expect you read the Popple story overnight, and that made you *think* you saw a hedgehog when you were only half awake," said Mrs. Norbury, hazarding a conjecture that probably came very near the truth.

Ada scouted the possibility of such a solution of her apparition.

"This must be hushed up," said Mrs. Norbury quickly; "the servants— "

"Hushed up!" exclaimed Ada, indignantly; "I'm writing a long report on it for the Research Society."

It was then that Hugo Norbury, who is not naturally a man of brilliant resource, had one of the really useful inspirations of his life.

"It was very wicked of us, Miss Bleek," he said, "but it would be a shame to let it go further. That white hedgehog is an old joke of ours; stuffed albino hedgehog, you know, that my father brought home from

Jamaica, where they grow to enormous size. We hide it in the room with a string on it, run one end of the string through the window; then we pull if from below and it comes scraping along the floor, just as you've described, and finally jerks out of the window. Taken in heaps of people; they all read up Popple and think it's old Harry Nicholson's ghost; we always stop them from writing to the papers about it, though. That would be carrying matters too far."

Mrs. Hatch-Mallard renewed the lease in due course, but Ada Bleek has never renewed her friendship.

THE MAPPINED LIFE

"THESE MAPPIN TERRACES at the Zoological Gardens are a great improvement on the old style of wild-beast cage," said Mrs. James Gurtleberry, putting down an illustrated paper; "they give one the illusion of seeing the animals in their natural surroundings. I wonder how much of the illusion is passed on to the animals?"

"That would depend on the animal," said her niece; "a jungle-fowl, for instance, would no doubt think its lawful jungle surroundings were faithfully reproduced if you gave it a sufficiency of wives, a goodly variety of seed food and ants' eggs, a commodious bank of loose earth to dust itself in, a convenient roosting tree, and a rival or two to make matters interesting. Of course there ought to be jungle-cats and birds of prey and other agencies of sudden death to add to the illusion of liberty, but the bird's own imagination is capable of inventing those—look how a domestic fowl will squawk an alarm note if a rook or wood pigeon passes over its run when it has chickens."

"You think, then, they really do have a sort of illusion, if you give them space enough—"

"In a few cases only. Nothing will make me believe that an acre or so of concrete enclosure will make up to a wolf or a tiger-cat for the range of night prowling that would belong to it in a wild state. Think of the dictionary of sound and scent and recollection that unfolds before a real wild beat as it comes out from its lair every evening, with the knowledge that in a few minutes it will be hieing along to some distant hunting ground where all the joy and fury of the chase awaits it; think of the crowded sensations of the brain when every rustle, every cry, every bent twig, and every whiff across the nostrils means something, something to do with life and death and dinner. Imagine the satisfaction of stealing down to your own particular drinking spot, choosing your own particular tree to scrape your claws on, finding your own particular bed of dried grass to roll on. Then, in the place of all that, put a concrete promenade, which will be of exactly the same dimensions whether you race or crawl across it, coated with stale, unvarying scents and surrounded with cries and noises that have ceased to have the least meaning or interest. As a substitute for a narrow cage the new enclosures are excellent, but I should think they are a poor imitation of a life of liberty."

"It's rather depressing to think that," said Mrs. Gurtleberry; "they look so spacious and so natural, but I suppose a good deal of what seems natural to us would be meaningless to a wild animal."

"That is where our superior powers of self-deception come in," said the niece; "we are able to live our unreal, stupid little lives on our particular Mappin terrace, and persuade ourselves that we really are untrammelled men and women leading a reasonable existence in a reasonable sphere."

"But good gracious," exclaimed the aunt, bouncing into an attitude of scandalised defence, "we are leading reasonable existences! What on earth do you mean by trammels? We are merely trammelled by the ordinary decent conventions of civilised society."

"We are trammelled," said the niece, calmly and pitilessly, "by restrictions of income and opportunity, and above all by lack of initiative. To some people a restricted income doesn't matter a bit, in fact it often seems to help as a means for getting a lot of reality out of life; I am sure there are men and women who do their shopping in little back streets of Paris, buying four carrots and a shred of beef for their daily sustenance, who lead a perfectly real and eventful existence. Lack of initiative is the thing that really cripples one, and that is where you and I and Uncle James are so hopelessly shut in. We are just so many animals stuck down on a Mappin terrace, with this difference in our disfavour, that the animals are there to be looked at, while nobody wants to look at us. As a matter of fact there would be nothing to look at. We get colds in winter and hay fever in summer, and if a wasp happens to sting one of us, well, that is the wasp's initiative, not ours; all we do is to wait for the swelling to go down. Whenever we do climb into local fame and notice, it is by indirect methods; if it happens to be a good flowering year for magnolias the neighbourhood observes: 'Have you seen the Gurtleberry's magnolia? It is a perfect mass of flowers,' and we go about telling people that there are fifty-seven blossoms as against thirty-nine the previous year."

"In Coronation year there were as many as sixty," put in the aunt, "your uncle has kept a record for the last eight years."

"Doesn't it ever strike you," continued the niece relentlessly, "that if we moved away from here or were blotted out of existence our local claim to fame would pass on automatically to whoever happened to take the house and garden? People would say to one another, 'Have you seen the Smith-Jenkins' magnolia? It is a perfect mass of flowers,' or else 'Smith-Jenkins tells me there won't be a single blossom on their magnolia this year; the east winds have turned all the buds black.' Now if, when we had gone, people still associated our names with the magnolia tree, no matter who temporarily possessed it, if they said, 'Ah, that's the tree on which the Gurtleberrys hung their cook because she sent up the wrong kind of sauce with the asparagus,' that would be something really due to our own initiative, apart from anything east winds or magnolia vitality might have to say in the matter."

"We should never do such a thing," said the aunt.

The niece gave a reluctant sigh.

"I can't imagine it," she admitted. "Of course," she continued, "there are heaps of ways of leading a real existence without committing sensational deeds of violence. It's the dreadful little everyday acts of pretended importance that give the Mappin stamp to our life. It would be entertaining, if it wasn't so pathetically tragic, to hear Uncle James fuss in here in the morning and announce, 'I must just go down into the town and find out what the men there are saying about Mexico. Matters are beginning to look serious there.' Then he patters away into the town, and talks in a highly serious voice to the tobacconist, incidentally buying an ounce of tobacco; perhaps he meets one or two others of the world's thinkers and talks to them in a highly serious voice, then he patters back here and announces with increased importance, 'I've just been talking to some men in the town about the condition of affairs in Mexico. They agree with the view that I have formed, that things there will have to get worse before they get better.' Of course nobody in the town cared in the least little bit what his views about Mexico were or whether he had any. The tobacconist wasn't even fluttered at his buying the ounce of tobacco; he knows that he purchases the same quantity of the same sort of tobacco every week. Uncle James might just as well have lain on his back in the garden and chattered to the lilac tree about the habits of caterpillars."

"I really will not listen to such things about your uncle," protested Mrs. James Gurtleberry angrily.

"My own case is just as bad and just as tragic," said the niece, dispassionately; "nearly everything about me is conventional make-believe. I'm not a good dancer, and no one could honestly call me good-looking, but when I go to one of our dull little local dances I'm conventionally supposed to 'have a heavenly time,' to attract the ardent homage of the local cavaliers, and to go home with my head awhirl with pleasurable recollections. As a matter of fact, I've merely put in some hours of indifferent dancing, drunk some badly-made claret cup, and listened to an enormous amount of laborious light conversation. A moonlight hen-stealing raid with the merry-eyed curate would be infinitely more exciting; imagine the pleasure of carrying off all those white minorcas that the Chibfords are always bragging about. When we had disposed of them we could give the proceeds to a charity, so there would be nothing really wrong about it. But nothing of that sort lies within the Mappined limits of my life. One of these days somebody dull and decorous and undistinguished will 'make himself agreeable' to me at a tennis party, as the saying is, and all the dull old gossips of the neighbourhood will begin to ask when we are to be engaged, and at last we shall be engaged, and people will give us butter-dishes and blotting-cases and framed pictures of young women feeding swans. Hullo, Uncle, are you going out?"

"I'm just going down to the town," announced Mr. James Gurtleberry, with an air of some importance: "I want to hear what people are saying about Albania. Affairs there are beginning to take on a very serious look. It's my opinion that we haven't seen the worst of things yet."

In this he was probably right, but there was nothing in the immediate or prospective condition of Albania to warrant Mrs. Gurtleberry in bursting into tears.

FATE

REX DILLOT was nearly twenty-four, almost good-looking and quite penniless. His mother was supposed to make him some sort of an allowance out of what her creditors allowed her, and Rex occasionally strayed into the ranks of those who earn fitful salaries as secretaries or companions to people who are unable to cope unaided with their correspondence or their leisure. For a few months he had been assistant editor and business manager of a paper devoted to fancy mice, but the devotion had been all on one side, and the paper disappeared with a certain abruptness from club reading-rooms and other haunts where it had made a gratuitous appearance. Still, Rex lived with some air of comfort and well-being, as one can live if one is born with a genius for that sort of thing, and a kindly Providence usually arranged that his weekend invitations coincided with the dates on which his one white dinner-waistcoat was in a laundry-returned condition of dazzling cleanness. He played most games badly, and was shrewd enough to recognise the fact, but he had developed a marvellously accurate judgement in estimating the play and chances of other people, whether in a golf match, billiard handicap, or croquet tournament. By dint of parading his opinion of such and such a player's superiority with a sufficient degree of youthful assertiveness he usually succeeded in provoking a wager at liberal odds, and he looked to his weekend winnings to carry him through the financial embarrassments of his mid-week existence. The trouble was, as he confided to Clovis Sangrail, that he never had enough available or even prospective cash at his command to enable him to fix the wager at a figure really worth winning.

"Some day," he said, "I shall come across a really safe thing, a bet that simply can't go astray, and then I shall put it up for all I'm worth, or rather for a good deal more than I'm worth if you sold me up to the last button."

"It would be awkward if it didn't happen to come off," said Clovis.

"It would be more than awkward," said Rex; "it would be a tragedy. All the same, it would be extremely amusing to bring it off. Fancy awaking in the morning with about three hundred pounds standing to one's credit. I should go and clear out my hostess's pigeon-loft before breakfast out of sheer good-temper."

"Your hostess of the moment mightn't have a pigeon-loft," said Clovis.

"I always choose hostesses that have," said Rex; "a pigeon-loft is indicative of a careless, extravagant, genial disposition, such as I like to see around me. People who strew corn broadcast for a lot of feathered inanities that just sit about cooing and giving each other the glad eye in a Louis Quatorze manner are pretty certain to do you well."

"Young Strinnit is coming down this afternoon," said Clovis reflectively; "I dare say you won't find it difficult to get him to back himself at billiards. He plays a pretty useful game, but he's not quite as good as he fancies he is."

"I know one member of the party who can walk round him," said Rex softly, an alert look coming into his eyes; "that cadaverous-looking Major who arrived last night. I've seen him play at St. Moritz. If I could get Strinnit to lay odds on himself against the Major the money would be safe in my pocket. This looks like the good thing I've been watching and praying for."

"Don't be rash," counselled Clovis, "Strinnit may play up to his self-imagined form once in a blue moon."

"I intend to be rash," said Rex quietly, and the look on his face corroborated his words.

"Are you all going to flock to the billiard-room?" asked Teresa Thundleford, after dinner, with an air of some disapproval and a good deal of annoyance. "I can't see what particular amusement you find in watching two men prodding little ivory balls about on a table."

"Oh, well," said her hostess, "it's a way of passing the time, you know."

"A very poor way, to my mind," said Mrs. Thundleford; "now I was going to have shown all of you the photographs I took in Venice last summer."

"You showed them to us last night," said Mrs. Cuvering hastily.

"Those were the ones I took in Florence. These are quite a different lot."

"Oh, well, some time tomorrow we can look at them. You can leave them down in the drawing-room, and then every one can have a look."

"I should prefer to show them when you are all gathered together, as I have quite a lot of explanatory remarks to make, about Venetian art and architecture, on the same lines as my remarks last night on the Florentine galleries. Also, there are some verses of mine that I should like to read you, on the rebuilding of the Campanile. But, of course, if you all prefer to watch Major Latton and Mr. Strinnit knocking balls about on a table—"

"They are both supposed to be first-rate players," said the hostess.

"I have yet to learn that my verses and my art causerie are of second-rate quality," said Mrs. Thundleford with acerbity. "However, as you all seem bent on watching a silly game, there's no more to be said. I shall go upstairs and finish some writing. Later on, perhaps, I will come down and join you."

To one, at least, of the onlookers the game was anything but silly. It was absorbing, exciting, exasperating, nerve-stretching, and finally it grew to be tragic. The Major with the St. Moritz reputation was playing a long way below his form, young Strinnit was playing slightly above his, and had all the luck of the game as well. From the very start the balls seemed possessed by a demon of contrariness; they trundled about complacently for one player, they would go nowhere for the other.

"A hundred and seventy, seventy-four," sang out the youth who was marking. In a game of two hundred and fifty up it was an enormous lead to hold. Clovis watched the flush of excitement die away from Dillot's face, and a hard white look take its place.

"How much have you go on?" whispered Clovis. The other whispered the sum through dry, shaking lips. It was more than he or any one connected with him could pay; he had done what he had said he would do. He had been rash.

"Two hundred and six, ninety-eight."

Rex heard a clock strike ten somewhere in the hall, then another somewhere else, and another, and another; the house seemed full of striking clocks. Then in the distance the stable clock chimed in. In another hour they would all be striking eleven, and he would be listening to them as a disgraced outcast, unable to pay, even in part, the wager he had challenged.

"Two hundred and eighteen, a hundred and three." The game was as good as over. Rex was as good as done for. He longed desperately for the ceiling to fall in, for the house to catch fire, for anything to happen that would put an end to that horrible rolling to and fro of red and white ivory that was jostling him nearer and nearer to his doom.

"Two hundred and twenty-eight, a hundred and seven."

Rex opened his cigarette-case; it was empty. That at least gave him a pretext to slip away from the room for the purpose of refilling it; he would spare himself the drawn-out torture of watching that hopeless game played out to the bitter end. He backed away from the circle of absorbed watchers and made his way up a short stairway to a long, silent corridor of bedrooms, each with a guests' name written in a little square on the door. In the hush that reigned in this part of the house he could still hear the hateful click-click of the balls; if he waited for a few minutes longer he would hear the little outbreak of clapping and buzz of congratulation that would hail Strinnit's victory. On the alert tension of his nerves there broke another sound, the aggressive, wrath-inducing breathing of one who sleeps in heavy after-dinner slumber. The sound came from a room just at his elbow; the card on the door bore the announcement "Mrs. Thundleford." The door was just slightly ajar; Rex pushed it open an inch or two more and looked in. The august Teresa had fallen asleep over an illustrated guide to Florentine art-galleries; at her side, somewhat dangerously near the edge of the table, was a reading-lamp. If Fate had been decently kind to him, thought Rex, bitterly, that lamp would have been knocked over by the sleeper and would have given them something to think of besides billiard matches.

There are occasions when one must take one's Fate in one's hands. Rex took the lamp in his.

"Two hundred and thirty-seven, one hundred and fifteen." Strinnit was at the table, and the balls lay in good position for him; he had a choice of two fairly easy shots, a choice which he was never to decide. A sudden hurricane of shrieks and a rush of stumbling feet sent every one flocking to the door. The Dillot boy crashed into the room, carrying in his arms the vociferous and somewhat dishevelled Teresa Thundleford; her clothing was certainly not a mass of flames, as the more excitable members of the party afterwards declared, but the edge of her skirt and part of the table-cover in which she had been hastily wrapped were alight in a flickering, half-hearted manner. Rex flung his struggling burden on the billiard table, and for one breathless minute the work of beating out the sparks with rugs and cushions and playing on them with soda-water syphons engrossed the energies of the entire company.

"It was lucky I was passing when it happened," panted Rex; "some one had better see to the room, I think the carpet is alight."

As a matter of fact the promptitude and energy of the rescuer had prevented any great damage being done, either to the victim or her surroundings. The billiard table had suffered most, and had to be laid up for repairs; perhaps it was not the best place to have chosen for the scene of salvage operations; but then, as Clovis remarked, when one is rushing about with a blazing woman in one's arms one can't stop to think out exactly where one is going to put her.

THE BULL

TOM YORKFIELD had always regarded his half-brother, Laurence, with a lazy instinct of dislike, toned down, as years went on, to a tolerant feeling of indifference. There was nothing very tangible to dislike him for; he was just a blood-relation, with whom Tom had no single taste or interest in common, and with whom, at the same time, he had had no occasion for quarrel. Laurence had left the farm early in life, and had lived for a few years on a small sum of money left him by his mother; he had taken up painting as a profession, and was reported to be doing fairly well at it, well enough, at any rate, to keep body and soul together. He specialised in painting animals, and he was successful in finding a certain number of people to buy his pictures. Tom felt a comforting sense of assured superiority in contrasting his position with that of his half-brother; Laurence was an artist-chap, just that and nothing more, though you might make it sound more important by calling an animal painter; Tom was a farmer, not in a very big way, it was true, but the Helsery farm had been in the family for some generations, and it had a good reputation for the stock raised on it. Tom had done his best, with the little capital at his command, to maintain and improve the standard of his small herd of cattle, and in Clover Fairy he had bred a bull which was something rather better than any that his immediate neighbours could show. It would not have made a sensation in the judging ring at an important cattle show, but it was as vigorous, shapely, and healthy a young animal as any small practical farmer could wish to possess. At the King's Head on market days Clover Fairy was very highly spoken of, and Yorkfield used to declare that he would not part with him for a hundred pounds; a hundred pounds is a lot of money in the small farming line, and probably anything over eighty would have tempted him.

It was with some especial pleasure that Tom took advantage of one of Laurence's rare visits to the farm to lead him down to the enclosure where Clover Fairy kept solitary state—the grass widower of a grazing harem. Tom felt some of his old dislike for his half-brother reviving; the artist was becoming more languid in his manner, more unsuitably turned-out in attire, and he seemed inclined to impart a slightly patronising tone to his conversation. He took no heed of a flourishing potato crop, but waxed enthusiastic over a clump of yellow-flowering weed that stood in a corner by a gateway, which was rather galling to the owner of a really very well weeded farm; again, when he might have been duly complimentary about a group of fat, black-faced lambs, that simply cried aloud for admiration, he became eloquent over the foliage tints of an oak copse on the hill opposite. But now he was being taken to inspect the crowning pride and glory of Helsery; however grudging he might be in his praises, however backward and niggardly with his congratulations, he would have to see and acknowledge the many excellences of that redoubtable animal. Some weeks ago, while on a business journey to Taunton, Tom had been invited by his half-brother to visit a studio in that town, where Laurence was exhibiting one of his pictures, a large canvas representing a bull standing knee-deep in some marshy ground; it had been good of its kind, no doubt, and Laurence had seemed inordinately pleased with it; "the best thing I've done yet," he had said over and over again, and Tom had generously agreed that it was fairly lifelike. Now, the man of pigments was going to be shown a real picture, a living model of strength and comeliness, a thing to feast the eyes on, a picture that exhibited new pose and action with every shifting minute, instead of standing glued into one unvarying attitude between the four walls of a frame. Tom unfastened a stout wooden door and led the way into a straw-bedded yard.

"Is he quiet?" asked the artist, as a young bull with a curly red coat came inquiringly towards them.

"He's playful at times," said Tom, leaving his half-brother to wonder whether the bull's ideas of play were of the catch-as-catch-can order. Laurence made one or two perfunctory comments on the animal's appearance and asked a question or so as to his age and such-like details; then he coolly turned the talk into another channel.

"Do you remember the picture I showed you at Taunton?" he asked.

"Yes," grunted Tom; "a white-faced bull standing in some slush.

Don't admire those Herefords much myself; bulky-looking brutes, don't seem to have much life in them. Daresay they're easier to paint that way; now, this young beggar is on the move all the time, aren't you, Fairy?"

"I've sold that picture," said Laurence, with considerable complacency in his voice.

"Have you?" said Tom; "glad to hear it, I'm sure. Hope you're pleased with what you've got for it."

"I got three hundred pounds for it," said Laurence.

Tom turned towards him with a slowly rising flush of anger in his face. Three hundred pounds! Under the most favourable market conditions that he could imagine his prized Clover Fairy would hardly fetch a hundred, yet here was a piece of varnished canvas, painted by his half-brother, selling for three times that sum. It was a cruel insult that went home with all the more force because it emphasised the triumph of the patronising, self-satisfied Laurence. The young farmer had meant to put his relative just a little out of conceit with himself by displaying the jewel of his possessions, and now the tables were turned, and his valued beast was made to look cheap and insignificant beside the price paid for a mere picture. It was so monstrously unjust; the painting would never be anything more than a dexterous piece of counterfeit life, while Clover Fairy was the real thing, a monarch in his little world, a personality in the countryside. After he was dead, even, he would still be something of a personality; his descendants would graze in those valley meadows and hillside pastures, they would fill stall and byre and milking-shed, their good red coats would speckle the landscape and crowd the marketplace; men would note a promising heifer or a well-proportioned steer, and say: "Ah, that one comes of good old Clover Fairy's stock." All that time the picture would be hanging, lifeless and unchanging, beneath its dust and varnish, a chattel that ceased to mean anything if you chose to turn it with its back to the wall. These thoughts chased themselves angrily through Tom Yorkfield's mind, but he could not put them into words. When he gave tongue to his feelings he put matters bluntly and harshly.

"Some soft-witted fools may like to throw away three hundred pounds on a bit of paintwork; can't say as I envy them their taste. I'd rather have the real thing than a picture of it."

He nodded towards the young bull, that was alternately staring at them with nose held high and lowering its horns with a half-playful, half-impatient shake of the head.

Laurence laughed a laugh of irritating, indulgent amusement.

"I don't think the purchaser of my bit of paintwork, as you call it, need worry about having thrown his money away. As I get to be better known and recognised my pictures will go up in value. That particular one will probably fetch four hundred in a sale-room five or six years hence; pictures aren't a bad investment if you know enough to pick out the work of the right men. Now you can't say your precious bull is going to get more valuable the longer you keep him; he'll have his little day, and then, if you go on keeping him, he'll come down at last to a few shillingsworth of hoofs and hide, just at a time, perhaps, when my bull is being bought for a big sum for some important picture gallery."

It was too much. The united force of truth and slander and insult put over heavy a strain on Tom Yorkfield's powers of restraint. In his right hand he held a useful oak cudgel, with his left he made a grab at the loose collar of Laurence's canary-coloured silk shirt. Laurence was not a fighting man; the fear of physical violence threw him off his balance as completely as overmastering indignation had thrown Tom off his, and thus it came to pass that Clover Fairy was regaled with the unprecedented sight of a human being scudding and squawking across the enclosure, like the hen that would persist in trying to establish a nesting-place in the manger. In another crowded happy moment the bull was trying to jerk Laurence over his left shoulder, to prod him in the ribs while still in the air, and to kneel on him when he reached the ground. It was only the vigorous intervention of Tom that induced him to relinquish the last item of his programme.

Tom devotedly and ungrudgingly nursed his half brother to a complete recovery from his injuries, which consisted of nothing more serious than a dislocated shoulder, a broken rib or two, and a little nervous prostration. After all, there was no further occasion for rancour in the young farmer's mind; Laurence's bull might sell for three hundred, or for six hundred, and be admired by thousands in some big picture gallery, but it would never toss a man over one shoulder and catch him a jab in the ribs before he had fallen on the other side. That was Clover Fairy's noteworthy achievement, which could never be taken away from him.

Laurence continues to be popular as an animal artist, but his subjects are always kittens or fawns or lambkins—never bulls.

MORLVERA

THE OLYMPIC Toy Emporium occupied a conspicuous frontage in an important West End street. It was happily named Toy Emporium, because one would never have dreamed of according it the familiar and yet pulse-quickening name of toyshop. There was an air of cold splendour and elaborate failure about the wares that were set out in its ample windows; they were the sort of toys that a tired shop-assistant displays and explains at Christmas time to exclamatory parents and bored, silent children. The animal toys looked more like natural history models than the comfortable, sympathetic companions that one would wish, at a certain age, to take to bed with one, and to smuggle into the bathroom. The mechanical toys incessantly did things that no one could want a toy to do more than a half a dozen times in its lifetime; it was a merciful reflection that in any right-minded nursery the lifetime would certainly be short.

Prominent among the elegantly-dressed dolls that filled an entire section of the window frontage was a large hobble-skirted lady in a confection of peach-coloured velvet, elaborately set off with leopard skin accessories, if one may use such a conveniently comprehensive word in describing an intricate feminine toilette. She lacked nothing that is to be found in a carefully detailed fashion-plate—in fact, she might be said to have something more than the average fashion-plate female possesses; in place of a vacant, expressionless stare she had character in her face. It must be admitted that it was bad character, cold, hostile, inquisitorial, with a sinister lowering of one eyebrow and a merciless hardness about the corners of the mouth. One might have imagined histories about her by the hour, histories in which unworthy ambition, the desire for money, and an entire absence of all decent feeling would play a conspicuous part.

As a matter of fact, she was not without her judges and biographers, even in this shop-window stage of her career. Emmeline, aged ten, and Bert, aged seven, had halted on the way from their obscure back street to the minnow-stocked water of St. James's Park, and were critically examining the hobble-skirted doll, and dissecting her character in no very tolerant spirit. There is probably a latent enmity between the necessarily under-clad and the unnecessarily over-dressed, but a little kindness and good fellowship on the part of the latter will often change the sentiment to admiring devotion; if the lady in peach-coloured velvet and leopard skin had worn a pleasant expression in addition to her other elaborate furnishings, Emmeline at least might have respected and even loved her. As it was, she gave her a horrible reputation, based chiefly on a second-hand knowledge of gilded depravity derived from the conversation of those who were skilled in the art of novelette reading; Bert filled in a few damaging details from his own limited imagination.

"She's a bad lot, that one is," declared Emmeline, after a long unfriendly stare; "'er 'usbind 'ates 'er."

"'E knocks 'er abart," said Bert, with enthusiasm.

"No, 'e don't, cos 'e's dead; she poisoned 'im slow and gradual, so that nobody didn't know. Now she wants to marry a lord, with 'eaps and 'eaps of money. 'E's got a wife already, but she's going to poison 'er, too."

"She's a bad lot," said Bert with growing hostility.

"'Er mother 'ates her, and she's afraid of 'er, too, cos she's got a serkestic tongue; always talking serkesms, she is. She's greedy, too; if there's fish going, she eats 'er own share and 'er little girl's as well, though the little girl is dellikit."

"She 'ad a little boy once," said Bert, "but she pushed 'im into the water when nobody wasn't looking."

"No she didn't," said Emmeline, "she sent 'im away to be kep' by poor people, so 'er 'usbind wouldn't know where 'e was. They ill-treat 'im somethink cruel."

"Wot's 'er nime?" asked Bert, thinking that it was time that so interesting a personality should be labelled.

"'Er nime?" said Emmeline, thinking hard, "'er nime's Morlvera." It was as near as she could get to the name of an adventuress who figured prominently in a cinema drama. There was silence for a moment while the possibilities of the name were turned over in the children's minds.

"Those clothes she's got on ain't paid for, and never won't be," said

Emmeline; "she thinks she'll get the rich lord to pay for 'em, but 'e won't. 'E's given 'er jools, 'underds of pounds' worth."

"'E won't pay for the clothes," said Bert, with conviction. Evidently there was some limit to the weak good nature of wealthy lords.

At that moment a motor carriage with liveried servants drew up at the emporium entrance; a large lady, with a penetrating and rather hurried manner of talking, stepped out, followed slowly and sulkily by a small boy, who had a very black scowl on his face and a very white sailor suit over the rest of him. The lady was continuing an argument which had probably commenced in Portman Square.

"Now, Victor, you are to come in and buy a nice doll for your cousin Bertha. She gave you a beautiful box of soldiers on your birthday, and you must give her a present on hers."

"Bertha is a fat little fool," said Victor, in a voice that was as loud as his mother's and had more assurance in it.

"Victor, you are not to say such things. Bertha is not a fool, and she is not in the least fat. You are to come in and choose a doll for her."

The couple passed into the shop, out of view and hearing of the two back-street children.

"My, he is in a wicked temper," exclaimed Emmeline, but both she and Bert were inclined to side with him against the absent Bertha, who was doubtless as fat and foolish as he had described her to be.

"I want to see some dolls," said the mother of Victor to the nearest assistant; "it's for a little girl of eleven."

"A fat little girl of eleven," added Victor by way of supplementary information.

"Victor, if you say such rude things about your cousin, you shall go to bed the moment we get home, without having any tea."

"This is one of the newest things we have in dolls," said the assistant, removing a hobble-skirted figure in peach-coloured velvet from the window; "leopard skin toque and stole, the latest fashion. You won't get anything newer than that anywhere. It's an exclusive design."

"Look!" whispered Emmeline outside; "they've bin and took Morlvera."

There was a mingling of excitement and a certain sense of bereavement in her mind; she would have liked to gaze at that embodiment of overdressed depravity for just a little longer.

"I 'spect she's going away in a kerridge to marry the rich lord," hazarded Bert.

"She's up to no good," said Emmeline vaguely.

Inside the shop the purchase of the doll had been decided on.

"It's a beautiful doll, and Bertha will be delighted with it," asserted the mother of Victor loudly.

"Oh, very well," said Victor sulkily; "you needn't have it stuck into a box and wait an hour while it's being done up into a parcel. I'll take it as it is, and we can go round to Manchester Square and give it to Bertha, and get the thing done with. That will save me the trouble of writing: 'For dear Bertha, with Victor's love,' on a bit of paper."

"Very well," said his mother, "we can go to Manchester Square on our way home. You must wish her many happy returns of tomorrow, and give her the doll."

"I won't let the little beast kiss me," stipulated Victor.

His mother said nothing; Victor had not been half as troublesome as she had anticipated. When he chose he could really be dreadfully naughty.

Emmeline and Bert were just moving away from the window when Morlvera made her exit from the shop, very carefully in Victor's arms. A look of sinister triumph seemed to glow in her hard, inquisitorial face. As for Victor, a certain scornful serenity had replaced the earlier scowls; he had evidently accepted defeat with a contemptuous good grace.

The tall lady gave a direction to the footman and settled herself in the carriage. The little figure in the white sailor suit clambered in beside her, still carefully holding the elegantly garbed doll.

The car had to be backed a few yards in the process of turning. Very stealthily, very gently, very mercilessly Victor sent Morlvera flying over his shoulder, so that she fell into the road just behind the retrogressing wheel. With a soft, pleasant-sounding scrunch the car went over the prostrate form, then it moved forward again with another scrunch. The carriage moved off and left Bert and Emmeline gazing in scared delight at a sorry mess of petrol-smeared velvet, sawdust, and leopard skin, which was all that remained of the hateful Morlvera. They gave a shrill cheer, and then raced away shuddering from the scene of so much rapidly enacted tragedy.

Later that afternoon, when they were engaged in the pursuit of minnows by the waterside in St. James's Park, Emmeline said in a solemn undertone to Bert—

"I've bin finking. Do you know oo 'e was? 'E was 'er little boy wot she'd sent away to live wiv poor folks. 'E come back and done that."

SHOCK TATICS

ON A late spring afternoon Ella McCarthy sat on a green-painted chair in Kensington Gardens, staring listlessly at an uninteresting stretch of park landscape, that blossomed suddenly into tropical radiance as an expected figure appeared in the middle distance.

"Hullo, Bertie!" she exclaimed sedately, when the figure arrived at the painted chair that was the nearest neighbour to her own, and dropped into it eagerly, yet with a certain due regard for the set of its trousers; "hasn't it been a perfect spring afternoon?"

The statement was a distinct untruth as far as Ella's own feelings were concerned; until the arrival of Bertie the afternoon had been anything but perfect.

Bertie made a suitable reply, in which a questioning note seemed to hover.

"Thank you ever so much for those lovely handkerchiefs," said Ella, answering the unspoken question; "they were just what I've been wanting. There's only one thing spoilt my pleasure in your gift," she added, with a pout.

"What was that?" asked Bertie anxiously, fearful that perhaps he had chosen a size of handkerchief that was not within the correct feminine limit.

"I should have liked to have written and thanked you for them as soon as I got them," said Ella, and Bertie's sky clouded at once.

"You know what mother is," he protested; "she opens all my letters, and if she found I'd been giving presents to any one there'd have been something to talk about for the next fortnight."

"Surely, at the age of twenty—" began Ella.

"I'm not twenty till September," interrupted Bertie.

"At the age of nineteen years and eight months," persisted Ella, "you might be allowed to keep your correspondence private to yourself."

"I ought to be, but things aren't always what they ought to be. Mother opens every letter that comes into the house, whoever it's for.

My sisters and I have made rows about it time and again, but she goes on doing it."

"I'd find some way to stop her if I were in your place," said Ella valiantly, and Bertie felt that the glamour of his anxiously deliberated present had faded away in the disagreeable restriction that hedged round its acknowledgment.

"Is anything the matter?" asked Bertie's friend Clovis when they met that evening at the swimming-bath.

"Why do you ask?" said Bertie.

"When you wear a look of tragic gloom in a swimming-bath," said Clovis, "it's especially noticeable from the fact that you're wearing very little else. Didn't she like the handkerchiefs?"

Bertie explained the situation.

"It is rather galling, you know," he added, "when a girl has a lot of things she wants to write to you and can't send a letter except by some roundabout, underhand way."

"One never realises one's blessings while one enjoys them," said Clovis; "now I have to spend a considerable amount of ingenuity inventing excuses for not having written to people."

"It's not a joking matter," said Bertie resentfully: "you wouldn't find it funny if your mother opened all your letters."

"The funny thing to me is that you should let her do it."

"I can't stop it. I've argued about it—"

"You haven't used the right kind of argument, I expect. Now, if every time one of your letters was opened you lay on your back on the dining-table during dinner and had a fit, or roused the entire family in the middle of the night to hear you recite one of Blake's *Poems of Innocence*, you would get a far more respectful hearing for future protests. People yield more consideration to a mutilated mealtime or a broken night's rest, than ever they would to a broken heart."

"Oh, dry up," said Bertie crossly, inconsistently splashing Clovis from head to foot as he plunged into the water.

It was a day or two after the conversation in the swimming-bath that a letter addressed to Bertie Heasant slid into the letter-box at his home, and thence into the hands of his mother. Mrs. Heasant was one of those empty-minded individuals to whom other people's affairs are perpetually interesting. The more private they are intended to be the more acute is the interest they arouse. She would have opened this particular letter in any case; the fact that it was marked "private," and diffused a delicate but penetrating aroma merely caused her to open it with headlong haste rather than matter-of-course deliberation. The harvest of sensation that rewarded her was beyond all expectations.

> Bertie, *carissimo*—
> I wonder if you will have the nerve to do it: it will take some nerve, too. Don't forget the jewels. They are a detail, but details interest me.
> Yours as ever,
> Clotilde.
>
> PS: Your mother must not know of my existence. If questioned swear you never heard of me.

For years Mrs. Heasant had searched Bertie's correspondence diligently for traces of possible dissipation or youthful entanglements, and at last the suspicions that had stimulated her inquisitorial zeal were justified by this one splendid haul. That any one wearing the exotic name "Clotilde" should write to Bertie under the incriminating announcement "as ever" was sufficiently electrifying, without the astounding allusion to the jewels. Mrs. Heasant could recall novels and dramas wherein jewels played an exciting and commanding role, and here, under her own roof, before her very eyes as it were, her own son was carrying on an intrigue in which jewels were merely an interesting detail. Bertie was not due home for another hour, but his sisters were available for the immediate unburdening of a scandal-laden mind.

"Bertie is in the toils of an adventuress," she screamed; "her name is Clotilde," she added, as if she thought they had better know the worst at once. There are occasions when more harm than good is done by shielding young girls from a knowledge of the more deplorable realities of life.

By the time Bertie arrived his mother had discussed every possible and improbable conjecture as to his guilty secret; the girls limited themselves to the opinion that their brother had been weak rather than wicked.

"Who is Clotilde?" was the question that confronted Bertie almost before he had got into the hall. His denial of any knowledge of such a person was met with an outburst of bitter laughter.

"How well you have learned your lesson!" exclaimed Mrs. Heasant. But satire gave way to furious indignation when she realised that Bertie did not intend to throw any further light on her discovery.

"You shan't have any dinner till you've confessed everything," she stormed.

Bertie's reply took the form of hastily collecting material for an impromptu banquet from the larder and locking himself into his bedroom. His mother made frequent visits to the locked door and shouted a succession of interrogations with the persistence of one who thinks that if you ask a question often enough an answer will eventually result. Bertie did nothing to encourage the supposition. An hour had passed in fruitless one-sided palaver when another letter addressed to Bertie and marked "private" made its appearance in the letter-box. Mrs. Heasant pounced on it with the enthusiasm of a cat that has missed its mouse and to whom a second has been unexpectedly vouchsafed. If she hoped for further disclosures assuredly she was not disappointed. It started abruptly:

> So you have really done it!
> Poor Dagmar. Now she is done for I almost pity her. You did it very well, you wicked boy, the servants all think it was suicide, and there will be no fuss. Better not touch the jewels till after the inquest.
> Clotilde.

Anything that Mrs. Heasant had previously done in the way of outcry was easily surpassed as she raced upstairs and beat frantically at her son's door.

"Miserable boy, what have you done to Dagmar?"

"It's Dagmar now, is it?" he snapped; "it will be Geraldine next."

"That it should come to this, after all my efforts to keep you at home of an evening," sobbed Mrs. Heasant; "it's no use you trying to hide things from me; Clotilde's letter betrays everything."

"Does it betray who she is?" asked Bertie; "I've heard so much about her, I should like to know something about her home-life. Seriously, if you go on like this I shall fetch a doctor; I've often enough been preached at about nothing, but I've never had an imaginary harem dragged into the discussion."

"Are these letters imaginary?" screamed Mrs. Heasant; "what about the jewels, and Dagmar, and the theory of suicide?"

No solution of these problems was forthcoming through the bedroom door, but the last post of the evening produced another letter for Bertie, and its contents brought Mrs. Heasant that enlightenment which had already dawned on her son.

Dear Bertie,

I hope I haven't distracted your brain with the spoof letters I've been sending in the name of a fictitious Clotilde. You told me the other day that the servants, or somebody at your home, tampered with your letters, so I thought I would give any one that opened them something exciting to read. The shock might do them good.

Yours,

Clovis Sangrail.

Mrs. Heasant knew Clovis slightly, and was rather afraid of him. It was not difficult to read between the lines of his successful hoax. In a chastened mood she rapped once more at Bertie's door.

"A letter from Mr. Sangrail. It's all been a stupid hoax. He wrote those other letters. Why, where are you going?"

Bertie had opened the door; he had on his hat and overcoat.

"I'm going for a doctor to come and see if anything's the matter with you. Of course it was all a hoax, but no person in his right mind could have believed all that rubbish about murder and suicide and jewels. You've been making enough noise to bring the house down for the last hour or two."

"But what was I to think of those letters?" whimpered Mrs. Heasant.

"I should have known what to think of them," said Bertie; "if you choose to excite yourself over other people's correspondence it's your own fault. Anyhow, I'm going for a doctor."

It was Bertie's great opportunity, and he knew it. His mother was conscious of the fact that she would look rather ridiculous if the story got about. She was willing to pay hush-money.

"I'll never open your letters again," she promised. And Clovis has no more devoted slave than Bertie Heasant.

THE SEVEN CREAM JUGS

"I SUPPOSE we shall never see Wilfred Pigeoncote here now that he has become heir to the baronetcy and to a lot of money," observed Mrs. Peter Pigeoncote regretfully to her husband.

"Well, we can hardly expect to," he replied, "seeing that we always choked him off from coming to see us when he was a prospective nobody. I don't think I've set eyes on him since he was a boy of twelve."

"There was a reason for not wanting to encourage his acquaintance-ship," said Mrs. Peter. "With that notorious failing of his he was not the sort of person one wanted in one's house."

"Well, the failing still exists, doesn't it?" said her husband; "or do you suppose a reform of character is entailed along with the estate?"

"Oh, of course, there is still that drawback," admitted the wife, "but one would like to make the acquaintance of the future head of the family, if only out of mere curiosity. Besides, cynicism apart, his being rich will make a difference in the way people will look at his failing. When a man is absolutely wealthy, not merely well-to-do, all suspicion of sordid motive naturally disappears; the thing becomes merely a tiresome malady."

Wilfrid Pigeoncote had suddenly become heir to his uncle, Sir Wilfrid Pigeoncote, on the death of his cousin, Major Wilfrid Pigeoncote, who had succumbed to the after-effects of a polo accident. (A Wilfrid Pigeoncote had covered himself with honours in the course of Marlborough's campaigns, and the name Wilfrid had been a baptismal weakness in the family ever since.) The new heir to the family dignity and estates was a young man of about five-and-twenty, who was known more by reputation than by person to a wide circle of cousins and kinsfolk. And the reputation was an unpleasant one. The numerous other Wilfrids in the family were distinguished one from another chiefly by the names of their residences or professions, as Wilfrid of Hubble-down, and young Wilfrid the Gunner, but this particular scion was known by the ignominious and expressive label of Wilfrid the Snatcher.

From his late schooldays onward he had been possessed by an acute and obstinate form of kleptomania; he had the acquisitive instinct of the collector without any of the collector's discrimination. Anything that was smaller and more portable than a sideboard, and above the value of ninepence, had an irresistible attraction for him, provided that it fulfilled the necessary condition of belonging to some one else. On the rare occasions when he was included in a country-house party, it was usual and almost necessary for his host, or some member of the family, to make a friendly inquisition through his baggage on the eve of his departure, to see if he had packed up "by mistake" any one else's property. The search usually produced a large and varied yield.

"This is funny," said Peter Pigeoncote to his wife, some half-hour after their conversation; "here's a telegram from Wilfrid, saying he's passing through here in his motor, and would like to stop and pay us his respects. Can stay for the night if it doesn't inconvenience us. Signed 'Wilfrid Pigeoncote.' Must be the Snatcher; none of the others have a motor. I suppose he's bringing us a present for the silver wedding."

"Good gracious!" said Mrs. Peter, as a thought struck her; "this is rather an awkward time to have a person with his failing in the house. All those silver presents set out in the drawing-room, and others coming by every post; I hardly know what we've got and what are still to come. We can't lock them all up; he's sure to want to see them."

"We must keep a sharp look-out, that's all," said Peter reassuringly.

"But these practised kleptomaniacs are so clever," said his wife, apprehensively, "and it will be so awkward if he suspects that we are watching him."

Awkwardness was indeed the prevailing note that evening when the passing traveller was being entertained. The talk flitted nervously and hurriedly from one impersonal topic to another. The guest had none of the furtive, half-apologetic air that his cousins had rather expected to find; he was polite, well-assured, and, perhaps, just a little inclined to "put on side". His hosts, on the other hand, wore an uneasy manner that might have been the hallmark of conscious depravity. In the drawing-room, after dinner, their nervousness and awkwardness increased.

"Oh, we haven't shown you the silver-wedding presents," said Mrs. Peter, suddenly, as though struck by a brilliant idea for entertaining the guest; "here they all are. Such nice, useful gifts. A few duplicates, of course."

"Seven cream jugs," put in Peter.

"Yes, isn't it annoying," went on Mrs. Peter; "seven of them. We feel that we must live on cream for the rest of our lives. Of course, some of them can be changed."

Wilfrid occupied himself chiefly with such of the gifts as were of antique interest, carrying one or two of them over to the lamp to examine their marks. The anxiety of his hosts at these moments resembled the solicitude of a cat whose newly born kittens are being handed round for inspection.

"Let me see; did you give me back the mustard-pot? This is its place here," piped Mrs. Peter.

"Sorry. I put it down by the claret-jug," said Wilfrid, busy with another object.

"Oh, just let me have the sugar-sifter again," asked Mrs. Peter, dogged determination showing through her nervousness; "I must label it who it comes from before I forget."

Vigilance was not completely crowned with a sense of victory. After they had said "Good-night" to their visitor, Mrs. Peter expressed her conviction that he had taken something.

"I fancy, by his manner, that there was something up," corroborated her husband; "do you miss anything?"

Mrs. Peters hastily counted the array of gifts.

"I can only make it thirty-four, and I think it should be thirty-five," she announced; "I can't remember if thirty-five includes the Archdeacon's cruet-stand that hasn't arrived yet."

"How on earth are we to know?" said Peter. "The mean pig hasn't brought us a present, and I'm hanged if he shall carry one off."

"Tomorrow, when's he having his bath," said Mrs. Peter excitedly, "he's sure to leave his keys somewhere, and we can go through his portmanteau. It's the only thing to do."

On the morrow an alert watch was kept by the conspirators behind half-closed doors, and when Wilfrid, clad in a gorgeous bath-robe, had made his way to the bathroom, there was a swift and furtive rush by two excited individuals towards the principal guest-chamber. Mrs. Peter kept guard outside, while her husband first made a hurried and successful search for the keys, and then plunged at the portmanteau with the air of a disagreeably conscientious Customs official. The quest was a brief one; a silver cream jug lay embedded in the folds of some zephyr shirts.

"The cunning brute," said Mrs. Peters; "he took a cream jug because there were so many; he thought one wouldn't be missed. Quick, fly down with it and put it back among the others."

Wilfrid was late in coming down to breakfast, and his manner showed plainly that something was amiss.

"It's an unpleasant thing to have to say," he blurted out presently, "but I'm afraid you must have a thief among your servants. Something's been taken out of my portmanteau. It was a little present from my mother and myself for your silver wedding. I should have given it to you last night after dinner, only it happened to be a cream jug, and you seemed annoyed at having so many duplicates, so I felt rather awkward about giving you another. I thought I'd get it changed for something else, and now it's gone."

"Did you say it was from your *mother* and yourself?" asked Mr. and Mrs. Peter almost in unison. The Snatcher had been an orphan these many years.

"Yes, my mother's at Cairo just now, and she wrote to me at Dresden to try and get you something quaint and pretty in the old silver line, and I pitched on this cream jug."

Both the Pigeoncotes had turned deadly pale. The mention of Dresden had thrown a sudden light on the situation. It was Wilfrid the Attache, a very superior young man, who rarely came within their social horizon, whom they had been entertaining unawares in the supposed character of Wilfrid the Snatcher. Lady Ernestine Pigeoncote, his mother, moved in circles which were entirely beyond their compass or ambitions, and the son would probably one day be an Ambassador. And they had rifled and despoiled his portmanteau! Husband and wife looked blankly and desperately at one another. It was Mrs. Peter who arrived first at an inspiration.

"How dreadful to think there are thieves in the house! We keep the drawing-room locked up at night, of course, but anything might be carried off while we are at breakfast."

She rose and went out hurriedly, as though to assure herself that the drawing-room was not being stripped of its silverware, and returned a moment later, bearing a cream jug in her hands.

"There are eight cream jugs now, instead of seven," she cried; "this one wasn't there before. What a curious trick of memory, Mr. Wilfrid! You must have slipped downstairs with it last night and put it there before we locked up, and forgotten all about having done it in the morning."

"One's mind often plays one little tricks like that," said Mr. Peter, with desperate heartiness. "Only the other day I went into the town to pay a bill, and went in again next day, having clean forgotten that I'd—"

"It is certainly the jug I bought for you," said Wilfrid, looking closely at it; "it was in my portmanteau when I got my bath-robe out this morning, before going to my bath, and it was not there when I unlocked the portmanteau on my return. Some one had taken it while I was away from the room."

The Pigeoncotes had turned paler than ever. Mrs. Peter had a final inspiration.

"Get me my smelling-salts, dear," she said to her husband; "I think they're in the dressing-room."

Peter dashed out of the room with glad relief; he had lived so long during the last few minutes that a golden wedding seemed within measurable distance.

Mrs. Peter turned to her guest with confidential coyness.

"A diplomat like you will know how to treat this as if it hadn't happened. Peter's little weakness; it runs in the family."

"Good Lord! Do you mean to say he's a kleptomaniac, like Cousin Snatcher?"

"Oh, not exactly," said Mrs. Peter, anxious to whitewash her husband a little greyer than she was painting him. "He would never touch anything he found lying about, but he can't resist making a raid on things that are locked up. The doctors have a special name for it. He must have pounced on your portmanteau the moment you went to your bath, and taken the first thing he came across. Of course, he had no motive for taking a cream jug; we've already got seven, as you know—not, of course, that we don't value the kind of gift you and your mother—hush here's Peter coming."

Mrs. Peter broke off in some confusion, and tripped out to meet her husband in the hall.

"It's all right," she whispered to him; "I've explained everything. Don't say anything more about it."

"Brave little woman," said Peter, with a gasp of relief; "I could never have done it."

*   *   *

Diplomatic reticence does not necessarily extend to family affairs. Peter Pigeoncote was never able to understand why Mrs. Consuelo van Bullyon, who stayed with them in the spring, always carried two very obvious jewel-cases with her to the bathroom, explaining them to any one she chanced to meet in the corridor as her manicure and face-massage set.

THE OCCASIONAL GARDEN

"DON'T TALK to me about town gardens," said Elinor Rapsley; "which means, of course, that I want you to listen to me for an hour or so while I talk about nothing else. 'What a nice-sized garden you've got,' people said to us when we first moved here. What I suppose they meant to say was what a nice-sized site for a garden we'd got. As a matter of fact, the size is all against it; it's too large to be ignored altogether and treated as a yard, and it's too small to keep giraffes in. You see, if we could keep giraffes or reindeer or some other species of browsing animal there we could explain the general absence of vegetation by a reference to the fauna of the garden: 'You can't have wapiti *and* Darwin tulips, you know, so we didn't put down any bulbs last year.' As it is, we haven't got the wapiti, and the Darwin tulips haven't survived the fact that most of the cats of the neighbourhood hold a parliament in the centre of the tulip bed; that rather forlorn looking strip that we intended to be a border of alternating geranium and spiraea has been utilised by the cat-parliament as a division lobby. Snap divisions seem to have been rather frequent of late, far more frequent than the geranium blooms are likely to be. I shouldn't object so much to ordinary cats, but I do complain of having a congress of vegetarian cats in my garden; they must be vegetarians, my dear, because, whatever ravages they may commit among the sweet pea seedlings, they never seem to touch the sparrows; there are always just as many adult sparrows in the garden on Saturday as there were on Monday, not to mention newly-fledged additions. There seems to have been an irreconcilable difference of opinion between sparrows and Providence since the beginning of time as to whether a crocus looks best standing upright with its roots in the earth or in a recumbent posture with its stem neatly severed; the sparrows always have the last word in the matter, at least in our garden they do. I fancy that Providence must have originally intended to bring in an amending Act, or whatever it's called, providing either for a less destructive sparrow or a more indestructible crocus. The one consoling point about our garden is that it's not visible from the drawing-room or the smoking-room, so unless people are dinning or lunching with us they can't spy out the nakedness of the land. That is why I am so furious with Gwenda Pottingdon, who has practically forced herself on me for lunch on Wednesday next; she heard me offer the Paulcote girl lunch if she was up shopping on that day, and, of course, she asked if she might come too. She is only coming to gloat over my bedraggled and flowerless borders and to sing the praises of her own detestably over-cultivated garden. I'm sick of being told that it's the envy of the neighbourhood; it's like everything else that belongs to her—her car, her dinner-parties, even her headaches, they are all superlative; no one else ever had anything like them. When her eldest child was confirmed it was such a sensational event, according to her account of it, that one almost expected questions to be asked about it in the House of Commons, and now she's coming on purpose to stare at my few miserable pansies and the gaps in my sweet-pea border, and to give me a glowing, full-length description of the rare and sumptuous blooms in her rose-garden."

"My dear Elinor," said the Baroness, "you would save yourself all this heart-burning and a lot of gardener's bills, not to mention sparrow anxieties, simply by paying an annual subscription to the O.O.S.A."

"Never heard of it," said Elinor; "what is it?"

"The Occasional-Oasis Supply Association," said the Baroness; "it exists to meet cases exactly like yours, cases of backyards that are of no practical use for gardening purposes, but are required to blossom into decorative scenic backgrounds at stated intervals, when a luncheon or dinner-party is contemplated. Supposing, for instance, you have people coming to lunch at one-thirty; you just ring up the Association at about ten o'clock the same morning, and say 'lunch garden'. That is all the trouble you have to take. By twelve forty-five your yard is carpeted with a strip of velvety turf, with a hedge of lilac or red may, or whatever happens to be in season, as a background, one or two cherry trees in blossom, and clumps of heavily-flowered rhododendrons filling in the odd corners; in the foreground you have a blaze of carnations or Shirley poppies, or tiger lilies in full bloom. As soon as the lunch is over and your guests have departed the garden departs also, and all the cats in Christendom can sit in council in your yard without causing you a moment's anxiety. If you have a bishop or an antiquary or something of that sort coming to lunch you just mention the fact when you are ordering the garden, and you get an old-world pleasaunce, with clipped yew hedges and a sundial and hollyhocks, and perhaps a mulberry tree, and borders of sweet-williams and Canterbury bells, and an oldfashioned beehive or two tucked away in a corner. Those are the ordinary lines of supply that the Oasis Association undertakes, but by paying a few guineas a year extra you are entitled to its emergency E.O.N. service."

"What on earth is an E.O.N. service?"

"It's just a conventional signal to indicate special cases like the incursion of Gwenda Pottingdon. It means you've got some one coming to lunch or dinner whose garden is alleged to be 'the envy of the neighbourhood.'"

"Yes," exclaimed Elinor, with some excitement, "and what happens then?"

"Something that sounds like a miracle out of the Arabian Nights. Your backyard becomes voluptuous with pomegranate and almond trees, lemon groves, and hedges of flowering cactus, dazzling banks of azaleas, marble-basined fountains, in which chestnut-and-white pond-herons step daintily amid exotic water-lilies, while golden pheasants strut about on alabaster terraces. The whole effect rather suggests the idea that Providence and Norman Wilkinson have dropped mutual jealousies and collaborated to produce a background for an open-air Russian Ballet; in point of fact, it is merely the background to your luncheon party. If there is any kick left in Gwenda Pottingdon, or whoever your E.O.N. guest of the moment may be, just mention carelessly that your climbing putella is the only one in England, since the one at Chatsworth died last winter. There isn't such a thing as a climbing putella, but Gwenda Pottingdon and her kind don't usually know one flower from another without prompting."

"Quick," said Elinor, "the address of the Association."

Gwenda Pottingdon did not enjoy her lunch. It was a simple yet elegant meal, excellently cooked and daintily served, but the piquant sauce of her own conversation was notably lacking. She had prepared a long succession of eulogistic comments on the wonders of her town garden, with its unrivalled effects of horticultural magnificence, and, behold, her theme was shut in on every side by the luxuriant hedge of Siberian berberis that formed a glowing background to Elinor's bewildering fragment of fairyland. The pomegranate and lemon trees, the terraced fountain, where golden carp slithered and wriggled amid the roots of gorgeous-hued irises, the banked masses of exotic blooms, the pagoda-like enclosure, where Japanese sand-badgers disported themselves, all these contributed to take away Gwenda's appetite and moderate her desire to talk about gardening matters.

"I can't say I admire the climbing putella," she observed shortly, "and anyway it's not the only one of its kind in England; I happen to know of one in Hampshire. How gardening is going out of fashion; I suppose people haven't the time for it nowadays."

Altogether it was quite one of Elinor's most successful luncheon parties.

It was distinctly an unforeseen catastrophe that Gwenda should have burst in on the household four days later at lunch-time and made her way unbidden into the dining-room.

"I thought I must tell you that my Elaine has had a watercolour sketch accepted by the Latent Talent Art Guild; it's to be exhibited at their summer exhibition at the Hackney Gallery. It will be the sensation of the moment in the art world—Hullo, what on earth has happened to your garden? It's not there!"

"Suffragettes," said Elinor promptly; "didn't you hear about it? They broke in and made hay of the whole thing in about ten minutes. I was so heart-broken at the havoc that I had the whole place cleared out; I shall have it laid out again on rather more elaborate lines."

"That," she said to the Baroness afterwards "is what I call having an emergency brain."

THE SHEEP

THE ENEMY had declared "no trumps." Rupert played out his ace and king of clubs and cleared the adversary of that suit; then the Sheep, whom the Fates had inflicted on him for a partner, took the third round with the queen of clubs, and, having no other club to lead back, opened another suit. The enemy won the remainder of the tricks—and the rubber.

"I had four more clubs to play; we only wanted the odd trick to win the rubber," said Rupert.

"But I hadn't another club to lead you," exclaimed the Sheep, with his ready, defensive smile.

"It didn't occur to you to throw your queen away on my king and leave me with the command of the suit," said Rupert, with polite bitterness.

"I suppose I ought to have—I wasn't certain what to do. I'm awfully sorry," said the Sheep.

Being awfully and uselessly sorry formed a large part of his occupation in life. If a similar situation had arisen in a subsequent hand he would have blundered just as certainly, and he would have been just as irritatingly apologetic.

Rupert stared gloomily across at him as he sat smiling and fumbling with his cards. Many men who have good brains for business do not possess the rudiments of a card-brain, and Rupert would not have judged and condemned his prospective brother-in-law on the evidence of his bridge play alone. The tragic part of it was that he smiled and fumbled through life just as fatuously and apologetically as he did at the card-table. And behind the defensive smile and the well-worn expressions of regret there shone a scarcely believable but quite obvious self-satisfaction. Every sheep of the pasture probably imagines that in an emergency it could become terrible as an army with banners—one has only to watch how they stamp their feet and stiffen their necks when a minor object of suspicion comes into view and behaves meekly. And probably the majority of human sheep see themselves in imagination taking great parts in the world's more impressive dramas, forming swift, unerring decisions in moments of crisis, cowing mutinies, allaying panics, brave, strong, simple, but, in spite of their natural modesty, always slightly spectacular.

"Why in the name of all that is unnecessary and perverse should Kathleen choose this man for her future husband?" was the question that Rupert asked himself ruefully. There was young Malcolm Athling, as nice-looking, decent, level-headed a fellow as any one could wish to meet, obviously her very devoted admirer, and yet she must throw herself away on this pale-eyed, weak-mouthed embodiment of self-approving ineptitude. If it had been merely Kathleen's own affair Rupert would have shrugged his shoulders and philosophically hoped that she might make the best of an undeniably bad bargain. But Rupert had no heir; his own boy lay underground somewhere on the Indian frontier, in goodly company. And the property would pass in due curse to Kathleen and Kathleen's husband. The Sheep would live there in the beloved old home, rearing up other little Sheep, fatuous and rabbit-faced and self-satisfied like himself, to dwell in the land and possess it. It was not a soothing prospect.

Towards dusk on the afternoon following the bridge experience Rupert and the Sheep made their way homeward after a day's mixed shooting. The Sheep's cartridge bag was nearly empty, but his game bag showed no signs of over-crowding. The birds he had shot at had seemed for the most part as impervious to death or damage as the hero of a melodrama. And for each failure to drop his bird he had some explanation or apology ready on his lips. Now he was striding along in front of his host, chattering happily over his shoulder, but obviously on the lookout for some belated rabbit or woodpigeon that might haply be secured as an eleventh-hour addition to his bag. As they passed the edge of a small copse a large bird rose from the ground and flew slowly towards the trees, offering an easy shot to the oncoming sportsmen. The Sheep banged forth with both barrels, and gave an exultant cry.

"Horray! I've shot a thundering big hawk!"

"To be exact, you've shot a honey-buzzard. That is the hen bird of one of the few pairs of honey-buzzards breeding in the United Kingdom. We've kept them under the strictest preservation for the last four years; every gamekeeper and village gun loafer for twenty miles round has been warned and bribed and threatened to respect their sanctity, and egg-snatching agents have been carefully guarded against during the breeding season. Hundreds of lovers of rare birds have delighted in seeing their snap-shotted portraits in Country Life, and now you've reduced the hen bird to a lump of broken feathers."

Rupert spoke quietly and evenly, but for a moment or two a gleam of positive hatred shone in his eyes.

"I say, I'm so sorry," said the Sheep, with his apologetic smile. "Of course I remember hearing about the buzzards, but somehow I didn't connect this bird with them. And it was such an east shot—"

"Yes," said Rupert; "that was the trouble."

Kathleen found him in the gun-room smoothing out the feathers of the dead bird. She had already been told of the catastrophe.

"What a horrid misfortune," she said sympathetically.

"It was my dear Robbie who first discovered them, the last time he was home on leave. Don't you remember how excited he was about them? Let's go and have some tea."

Both bridge and shooting were given a rest for the next two or three weeks. Death, who enters into no compacts with party whips, had forced a Parliamentary vacancy on the neighbourhood at the least convenient season, and the local partisans on either side found themselves immersed in the discomforts of a mid-winter election. Rupert took his politics seriously and keenly. He belonged to that type of strangely but rather happily constituted individuals which these islands seem to produce in a fair plenty; men and women who for no personal profit or gain go forth from their comfortable firesides or club card-rooms to hunt to and fro in the mud and rain and wind for the capture or tracking of a stray vote here and there on their party's behalf—not because they think they ought to, but because they want to. And his energies were welcome enough on this occasion, for the seat was a closely disputed possession, and its loss or retention would count for much in the present position of the Parliamentary game. With Kathleen to help him, he had worked his corner of the constituency with tireless, well-directed zeal, taking his share of the dull routine work as well as of the livelier episodes. The talking part of the campaign wound up on the eve of the poll with a meeting in a centre where more undecided votes were supposed to be concentrated than anywhere else in the division. A good final meeting here would mean everything. And the speakers, local and imported, left nothing undone to improve the occasion. Rupert was down for the unimportant task of moving the complimentary vote to the chairman which should close the proceedings.

"I'm so hoarse," he protested, when the moment arrived; "I don't believe I can make my voice heard beyond the platform."

"Let me do it," said the Sheep; "I'm rather good at that sort of thing."

The chairman was popular with all parties, and the Sheep's opening words of complimentary recognition received a round of applause. The orator smiled expansively on his listeners and seized the opportunity to add a few words of political wisdom on his own account. People looked at the clock or began to grope for umbrellas and discarded neckwraps. Then, in the midst of a string of meaningless platitudes, the Sheep delivered himself of one of those blundering remarks which travel from one end of a constituency to the other in half an hour, and are seized on by the other side as being more potent on their behalf than a ton of election literature. There was a general shuffling and muttering across the length and breadth of the hall, and a few hisses made themselves heard. The Sheep tried to whittle down his remark, and the chairman unhesitatingly threw him over in his speech of thanks, but the damage was done.

"I'm afraid I lost touch with the audience rather over that remark," said the Sheep afterwards, with his apologetic smile abnormally developed.

"You lost us the election," said the chairman, and he proved a true prophet.

A month or so of winter sport seemed a desirable pick-me-up after the strenuous work and crowning discomfiture of the election. Rupert

and Kathleen hied them away to a small Alpine resort that was just coming into prominence, and thither the Sheep followed them in due
course, in his role of husband-elect. The wedding had been fixed for the
end of March.

It was a winter of early and unseasonable thaws, and the far end of
the local lake, at a spot where swift currents flowed into it, was decorated
with notices, written in three languages, warning skaters not to venture
over certain unsafe patches. The folly of approaching too near these danger spots seemed to have a natural fascination for the Sheep.

"I don't see what possible danger there can be," he protested, with
his inevitable smile, when Rupert beckoned him away from the pro-
scribed area; "the milk that I put out on my window-sill last night was
frozen an inch deep."

"It hadn't got a strong current flowing through it," said Rupert; "in
any case, there is not much sense in hovering round a doubtful piece of
ice when there are acres of good ice to skate over. The secretary of the ice-
committee has warned you once already."

A few minutes later Rupert heard a loud squeal of fear, and saw a
dark spot blotting the smoothness of the lake's frozen surface. The Sheep
was struggling helplessly in an ice-hole of his own making. Rupert gave
one loud curse, and then dashed full tilt for the shore; outside a low stable building on the lake's edge he remembered having seen a ladder. If he
could slide it across the ice-hole before the Sheep went under the rescue
would be comparatively simple work. Other skaters were dashing up
from a distance, and, with the ladder's help, they could get him out of
his deathtrap without having to trust themselves on the margin of rotten
ice. Rupert sprang on to the surface of lumpy, frozen snow, and stag-
gered to where the ladder lay. He had already lifted it when the rattle of a
chain and a furious outburst of growls burst on his hearing, and he was
dashed to the ground by a mass of white and tawny fur. A sturdy young
yard-dog, frantic with the pleasure of performing his first piece of actice
guardian service, was ramping and snarling over him, rendering the task
of regaining his feet or securing the ladder a matter of considerable difficulty. When he had at last succeeded in both efforts he was just by a

hair's-breadth too late to be of any use. The Sheep had definitely disappeared under the ice-rift.

Kathleen Athling and her husband stay the greater part of the year with Rupert, and a small Robbie stands in some danger of being idolised by a devoted uncle. But for twelve months of the year Rupert's most inseparable and valued companion is a sturdy tawny and white yard-dog.

THE OVERSIGHT

"IT'S LIKE a Chinese puzzle," said Lady Prowche resentfully, staring at a scribbled list of names that spread over two or three loose sheets of note-paper on her writing-table. Most of the names had a pencil mark running through them.

"What is like a Chinese puzzle?" asked Lena Luddleford briskly; she rather prided herself on being able to grapple with the minor problems of life.

"Getting people suitably sorted together. Sir Richard likes me to have a house party about this time of year, and gives me a free hand as to whom I should invite; all he asks is that it should be a peaceable party, with no friction or unpleasantness."

"That seems reasonable enough," said Lena.

"Not only reasonable, my dear, but necessary. Sir Richard has his literary work to think of; you can't expect a man to concentrate on the tribal disputes of Central Asian clansmen when he's got social feuds blazing under his own roof."

"But why should they blaze? Why should there be feuds at all within the compass of a house party?"

"Exactly; why should they blaze or why should they exist?" echoed Lady Prowche; "the point is that they always do. We have been unlucky; persistently unlucky, now that I come to look back on things. We have always got people of violently opposed views under one roof, and the result has been not merely unpleasantness but explosion."

"Do you mean people who disagree on matters of political opinion and religious views?" asked Lena.

"No, not that. The broader lines of political or religious difference don't matter. You can have Church of England and Unitarian and Buddhist under the same roof without courting disaster; the only Buddhist I ever had down here quarrelled with everybody, but that was on account of his naturally squabblesome temperament; it had nothing to do with his religion. And I've always found that people can differ profoundly about politics and meet on perfectly good terms at breakfast. Now, Miss Larbor Jones, who was staying here last year, worships Lloyd George as a sort of wingless angel, while Mrs. Walters, who was down here at the same time, privately considers him to be—an antelope, let us say."

"An antelope?"

"Well, not an antelope exactly, but something with horns and hoofs and tail."

"Oh, I see."

"Still, that didn't prevent them from being the chummiest of mortals on the tennis court and in the billiard-room. They did quarrel finally, about a lead in a doubled hand of no-trumps, but that of course is a thing that no account of judicious guest-grouping could prevent. Mrs. Walters had got king, knave, ten, and seven of clubs—"

"You were saying that there were other lines of demarcation that caused the bother," interrupted Lena.

"Exactly. It is the minor differences and side issues that give so much trouble," said Lady Prowche; "not to my dying day shall I forget last year's upheaval over the Suffragette question. Laura Henniseed left the house in a state of speechless indignation, but before she had reached that state she had used language that would not have been tolerated in the Austrian Reichsrath. Intensive bear-gardening was Sir Richard's description of the whole affair, and I don't think he exaggerated."

"Of course the Suffragette question is a burning one, and lets loose the most dreadful ill-feeling," said Lena; "but one can generally find out beforehand what people's opinions—"

"My dear, the year before it was worse. It was Christian Science. Selina Goobie is a sort of High Priestess of the Cult, and she put down all opposition with a high hand. Then one evening, after dinner, Clovis Sangrail put a wasp down her back, to see if her theory about the non-existence of pain could be depended on in an emergency. The wasp was small, but very efficient, and it had been soured in temper by being kept in a paper cage all the afternoon. Wasps don't stand confinement well, at least this one didn't. I don't think I ever realised till that moment what the word 'invective' could be made to mean. I sometimes wake in the night and think I still hear Selina describing Clovis's conduct and general character. That was the year that Sir Richard was writing his volume on *Domestic Life in Tartary*. The critics all blamed it for a lack of concentration."

"He's engaged on a very important work this year, isn't he?" asked Lena.

" 'Land-tenure in Turkestan,' " said Lady Prowche; "he is just at work on the final chapters and they require all the concentration he can give them. That is why I am so very anxious not to have any unfortunate disturbance this year. I have taken every precaution I can think of to bring non-conflicting and harmonious elements together; the only two people I am not quite easy about are the Atkinson man and Marcus Popham. They are the two who will be down here longest together, and if they are going to fall foul of one another about any burning question, well, there will be more unpleasantness."

"Can't you find out anything about them? About their opinions, I mean."

"Anything? My dear Lena, there's scarcely anything that I haven't found out about them. They're both of them moderate Liberal, Evangelical, mildly opposed to female suffrage, they approve of the Falconer Report, and the Stewards' decision about Craganour. Thank goodness in this country we don't fly into violent passions about Wagner and Brahms and things of that sort. There is only one thorny subject that I haven't been able to make sure about, the only stone that I have left unturned. Are they unanimously anti-vivisectionist or do they both uphold the necessity for scientific experiment? There has been a lot of correspondence on the subject in our local newspapers of late, and the vicar is certain to preach a sermon about it; vicars are dreadfully provocative at times. Now, if you could only find out for me whether these two men are divergently for or against—"

"I!" exclaimed Lena; "how am I to find out? I don't know either of them to speak to."

"Still you might discover, in some roundabout way. Write to them, under as assumed name of course, for subscriptions to one or other cause—or, better still, send a stamped typewritten reply postcard, with a request for a declaration for or against vivisection; people who would hesitate to commit themselves to a subscription will cheerfully write Yes or No on a prepaid postcard. If you can't manage it that way, try and meet them at some one's house and get into argument on the subject. I think Milly occasionally has one or other of them at her at-homes; you might have the luck to meet both of them there the same evening. Only it must be done soon. My invitations ought to go out by Wednesday or Thursday at the latest, and today is Friday.

"Milly's at-homes are not very amusing, as a rule," said Lena, "and one never gets a chance of talking uninterruptedly to any one for a couple of minutes at a time; Milly is one of those restless hostesses who always seem to be trying to see how you look in different parts of the room, in fresh grouping effects. Even if I got to speak to Popham or Atkinson I couldn't plunge into a topic like vivisection straight away. No, I think the postcard scheme would be more hopeful and decidedly less tiresome. How would it be best to word them?"

"Oh, something like this: 'Are you in favour of experiments on living animals for the purpose of scientific research—Yes or No?' That is quite simple and unmistakable. If they don't answer it will at least be an indication that they are indifferent about the subject, and that is all I want to know."

"All right," said Lena, "I'll get my brother-in-law to let me have them addressed to his office, and he can telephone the result of the plebiscite direct to you."

"Thank you ever so much," said Lady Prowche gratefully, "and be sure to get the cards sent off as soon as possible."

On the following Tuesday the voice of an office clerk, speaking through the telephone, informed Lady Prowche that the postcard poll showed unanimous hostility to experiments on living animals.

Lady Prowche thanked the office clerk, and in a louder and more fervent voice she thanked Heaven. The two invitations, already sealed and addressed, were immediately dispatched; in due course they were both accepted. The house party of the halcyon hours, as the prospective hostess called it, was auspiciously launched.

Lena Luddleford was not included among the guests, having previously committed herself to another invitation. At the opening day of a cricket festival, however, she ran across Lady Prowche, who had motored over from the other side of the county. She wore the air of one who is not interested in cricket and not particularly interested in life. She shook hands limply with Lena, and remarked that it was a beastly day.

"The party, how has it gone off?" asked Lena quickly.

"Don't speak of it!" was the tragical answer; "why do I always have such rotten luck?"

"But what has happened?"

"It has been awful. Hyaenas could not have behaved with greater savagery. Sir Richard said so, and he has been in countries where hyaenas live, so he ought to know. They actually came to blows!"

"Blows?"

"Blows and curses. It really might have been a scene from one of Hogarth's pictures. I never felt so humiliated in my life. What the servants must have thought!"

"But who were the offenders?"

"Oh, naturally the very two that we took all the trouble about."

"I thought they agreed on every subject that one could violently disagree about—religion, politics, vivisection, the Derby decision, the Falconer Report; what else was there left to quarrel about?"

"My dear, we were fools not to have thought of it. One of them was Pro-Greek and the other Pro-Bulgar."

HYACINTH

"THE NEW fashion of introducing the candidate's children into an election contest is a pretty one," said Mrs. Panstreppon; "it takes away something from the acerbity of party warfare, and it makes an interesting experience for children to look back on in after years. Still, if you will listen to my advice, Matilda, you will not take Hyacinth with you down to Luffbridge on election day."

"Not take Hyacinth!" exclaimed his mother; "but why not? Jutterly is bringing his three children, and they are going to drive a pair of Nubian donkeys about the town, to emphasise the fact that their father has been appointed Colonial Secretary. We are making the demand for a strong Navy a special feature in our campaign, and it will be particularly appropriate to have Hyacinth dressed in his sailor suit. He'll look heavenly."

"The question is, not how he'll look, but how he'll behave. He's a delightful child, of course, but there is a strain of unbridled pugnacity in him that breaks out at times in a really alarming fashion. You may have forgotten the affair of the little Gaffin children; I haven't."

"I was in India at the time, and I've only a vague recollection of what happened; he was very naughty, I know."

"He was in his goat-carriage, and met the Gaffins in their perambulator, and he drove the goat full tilt at them and sent the perambulator spinning. Little Jacky Gaffin was pinned down under the wreckage, and while the nurse had her hands full with the goat Hyacinth was laying into Jacky's legs with his belt like a small fury."

"I'm not defending him," said Matilda, "but they must have done something to annoy him."

"Nothing intentionally, but some one had unfortunately told him that they were half French—their mother was a Duboc, you know—and he had been having a history lesson that morning, and had just heard of the final loss of Calais by the English, and was furious about it. He said he'd teach the little toads to go snatching towns from us, but we didn't know at the time that he was referring to the Gaffins. I told him after-wards that all bad feeling between the two nations had died out long ago, and that anyhow the Gaffins were only half French, and he said that it was only the French half of Jacky that he had been hitting; the rest had been buried under the perambulator. If the loss of Calais unloosed such fury in him, I tremble to think what the possible loss of the election might entail."

"All that happened when he was eight; he's older now and knows better."

"Children with Hyacinth's temperament don't know better as they grow older; they merely know more."

"Nonsense. He will enjoy the fun of the election, and in any case he'll be tired out by the time the poll is declared, and the new sailor suit that I've had made for him is just in the right shade of blue for our election colours, and it will exactly match the blue of his eyes. He will be a perfectly charming note of colour."

"There is such a thing as letting one's aesthetic sense override one's moral sense," said Mrs. Panstreppon. "I believe you would have con-doned the South Sea Bubble and the persecution of the Albigenses if they had been carried out in effective colour schemes. However, if any-thing unfortunate should happen down at Luffbridge, don't say it wasn't foreseen by one member of the family."

The election was keenly but decorously contested. The newly-appointed Colonial Secretary was personally popular, while the Government to which he adhered was distinctly unpopular, and there was some expectancy that the majority of four hundred, obtained at the last elec-tion, would be altogether wiped out. Both sides were hopeful, but nei-ther could feel confident. The children were a great success; the little Jutterlys drove their chubby donkeys solemnly up and down the main streets, displaying posters which advocated the claims of their father on the broad general grounds that he was their father, while as for Hyacinth, his conduct might have served as a model for any seraph-child that had strayed unwittingly on to the scene of an electoral contest. Of his own accord, and under the delighted eyes of half a dozen camera operators, he had gone up to the Jutterly children and presented them with a packet of butterscotch; "we needn't be enemies because we're wearing the opposite colours," he said with engaging friendliness, and the occupants of the donkey-cart accepted his offering with polite solemnity. The grown-up members of both political camps were delighted at the incident—with the exception of Mrs. Panstreppon, who shuddered.

"Never was Clytemnestra's kiss sweeter than on the night she slew me," she quoted, but made the quotation to herself.

The last hour of the poll was a period of unremitting labour for both parties; it was generally estimated that not more than a dozen votes separated the candidates, and every effort was made to bring up obstinately wavering electors. It was with a feeling of relaxation and relief that every one heard the clocks strike the hour for the close of the poll. Exclamations broke out from the tired workers, and corks flew out from bottles.

"Well, if we haven't won; we've done our level best." "It has been a clean straight fight, with no rancour." "The children were quite a charming feature, weren't they?"

The children? It suddenly occurred to everybody that they had seen nothing of the children for the last hour. What had become of the three little Jutterlys and their donkey-cart, and, for the matter of that, what had become of Hyacinth. Hurried, anxious embassies went backwards and forwards between the respective party headquarters and the various committee-rooms, but there was blank ignorance everywhere as to the whereabouts of the children. Every one had been too busy in the closing moments of the poll to bestow a thought on them. Then there came a telephone call at the Unionist Women's Committee-rooms, and the voice of Hyacinth was heard demanding when the poll would be declared.

"Where are you, and where are the Jutterly children?" asked his mother.

"I've just finished having high-tea at a pastry-cook's," came the answer, "and they let me telephone. I've had a poached egg and a sausage roll and four meringues."

"You'll be ill. Are the little Jutterlys with you?"

"Rather not. They're in a pigstye."

"A pigstye? Why? What pigstye?"

"Near the Crawleigh Road. I met them driving about a back road, and told them they were to have tea with me, and put their donkeys in a yard that I knew of. Then I took them to see an old sow that had got ten little pigs. I got the sow into the outer stye by giving her bits of bread, while the Jutterlys went in to look at the litter, then I bolted the door and left them there."

"You wicked boy, do you mean to say you've left those poor children there alone in the pigstye?"

"They're not alone, they've got ten little pigs in with them; they're jolly well crowded. They were pretty mad at being shut in, but not half as mad as the old sow is at being shut out from her young ones. If she gets in while they're there she'll bite them into mincemeat. I can get them out by letting a short ladder down through the top window, and that's what I'm going to do *if we win*. If their blighted father gets in, I'm just going to open the door for the sow, and let her do what she dashed well likes to them. That's why I want to know when the poll will be declared."

Here the narrator rang off. A wild stampede and a frantic sending-off of messengers took place at the other end of the telephone. Nearly all the workers on either side had disappeared to their various club-rooms and public-house bars to await the declaration of the poll, but enough local information could be secured to determine the scene of Hyacinth's exploit. Mr. John Ball had a stable yard down near the Crawleigh Road, up a short lane, and his sow was known to have a litter of ten young ones. Thither went in headlong haste both the candidates, Hyacinth's mother, his aunt (Mrs. Panstreppon), and two or three hurriedly-summoned friends. The two Nubian donkeys, contentedly munching at bundles of hay, met their gaze as they entered the yard. The hoarse savage grunting of an enraged animal and the shriller note of thirteen young voices, three of them human, guided them to the stye, in the outer yard of which a huge Yorkshire sow kept up a ceaseless raging patrol before a closed door. Reclining on the broad ledge of an open window, from which point of vantage he could reach down and shoot the bolt of the door, was Hyacinth, his blue sailor-suit somewhat the worse of wear, and his angel smile exchanged for a look of demoniacal determination.

"If any of you come a step nearer," he shouted, "the sow will be inside in half a jiffy."

A storm of threatening, arguing, entreating expostulation broke from the baffled rescue party, but it made no more impression on Hyacinth than the squealing tempest that raged within the stye.

"If Jutterly heads the poll I'm going to let the sow in. I'll teach the blighters to win elections from us."

"He means it," said Mrs. Panstreppon; "I feared the worst when I saw that butterscotch incident."

"It's all right, my little man," said Jutterly, with the duplicity to which even a Colonial Secretary can sometimes stoop, "your father has been elected by a large majority."

"Liar!" retorted Hyacinth, with the directness of speech that is not merely excusable, but almost obligatory, in the political profession; "the votes aren't counted yet. You won't gammon me as to the result, either. A boy that I've palled with is going to fire a gun when the poll is declared; two shots if we've won, one shot if we haven't."

The situation began to look critical. "Drug the sow," whispered Hyacinth's father.

Some one went off in the motor to the nearest chemist's shop and returned presently with two large pieces of bread, liberally dosed with narcotic. The bread was thrown deftly and unostentatiously into the stye, but Hyacinth saw through the manoeuvre. He set up a piercing imitation of a small pit in Purgatory, and the infuriated mother ramped round and round the stye; the pieces of bread were trampled into slush.

At any moment now the poll might be declared. Jutterly flew back to the Town Hall, where the votes were being counted. His agent met him with a smile of hope.

"You're eleven ahead at present, and only about eighty more to be counted; you're just going to squeak through."

"I mustn't squeak through," exclaimed Jutterly, hoarsely. "You must object to every doubtful vote on our side that can possibly be disallowed. I must *not* have the majority."

Then was seen the unprecedented sight of a party agent challenging the votes on his own side with a captiousness that his opponents would have hesitated to display. One or two votes that would have certainly passed muster under ordinary circumstances were disallowed, but even so Jutterly was six ahead with only thirty more to be counted.

To the watchers by the stye the moments seemed intolerable. As a last resort some one had been sent for a gun with which to shoot the sow, though Hyacinth would probably draw the bolt the moment such a weapon was brought into the yard. Nearly all the men were away from their homes, however, on election night, and the messenger had evidently gone far afield in his search. It must be a matter of minutes now to the declaration of the poll.

A sudden roar of shouting and cheering was heard from the direction of the Town Hall. Hyacinth's father clutched a pitchfork and prepared to dash into the stye in the forlorn hope of being in time.

A shot rang out in the evening air. Hyacinth stooped down from his perch and put his finger on the bolt. The sow pressed furiously against the door.

"Bang," came another shot.

Hyacinth wriggled back, and sent a short ladder down through the window of the inner stye.

"Now you can come up, you unclean little blighters," he sang out; "my daddy's got in, not yours. Hurry up, I can't keep the sow waiting much longer. And don't you jolly well come butting into any election again where I'm on the job."

In the reaction that set in after the deliverance furious recrimination were indulged in by the lately opposed candidates, their women folk, agents, and party helpers. A recount was demanded, but failed to establish the fact that the Colonial Secretary had obtained a majority. Altogether the election left a legacy of soreness behind it, apart from any that was experienced by Hyacinth in person.

"It is the last time I shall let him go to an election," exclaimed his mother.

"There I think you are going to extremes," said Mrs. Panstreppon; "if there should be a general election in Mexico I think you might safely let him go there, but I doubt whether our English politics are suited to the rough and tumble of an angel-child."

THE IMAGE OF THE LOST SOLE

THERE WERE a number of carved stone figures placed at intervals along the parapets of the old Cathedral; some of them represented angels, others kings and bishops, and nearly all were in attitudes of pious exaltation and composure. But one figure, low down on the cold north side of the building, had neither crown, mitre, not nimbus, and its face was hard and bitter and downcast; it must be a demon, declared the fat blue pigeons that roosted and sunned themselves all day on the ledges of the parapet; but the old belfry jackdaw, who was an authority on ecclesiastical architecture, said it was a lost soul. And there the matter rested.

One autumn day there fluttered on to the Cathedral roof a slender, sweet-voiced bird that had wandered away from the bare fields and thinning hedgerows in search of a winter roosting-place. It tried to rest its tired feet under the shade of a great angel-wing or to nestle in the sculptured folds of a kingly robe, but the fat pigeons hustled it away from wherever it settled, and the noisy sparrow-folk drove it off the ledges. No respectable bird sang with so much feeling, they cheeped one to another, and the wanderer had to move on.

Only the effigy of the Lost Soul offered a place of refuge. The pigeons did not consider it safe to perch on a projection that leaned so much out of the perpendicular, and was, besides, too much in the shadow. The figure did not cross its hands in the pious attitude of the other graven dignitaries, but its arms were folded as in defiance and their angle made a snug resting-place for the little bird. Every evening it crept trustfully into its corner against the stone breast of the image, and the darkling eyes seemed to keep watch over its slumbers. The lonely bird grew to love its lonely protector, and during the day it would sit from time to time on some rainshoot or other abutment and trill forth its sweetest music in grateful thanks for its nightly shelter. And, it may have been the work of wind and weather, or some other influence, but the wild drawn face seemed gradually to lose some of its hardness and unhappiness. Every day, through the long monotonous hours, the song of his little guest would come up in snatches to the lonely watcher, and at evening, when the vesper-bell was ringing and the great grey bats slid out of their hiding-places in the belfry roof, the bright-eyed bird would return, twitter a few sleepy notes, and nestle into the arms that were waiting for him. Those were happy days for the Dark Image. Only the great bell of the Cathedral rang out daily its mocking message, "After joy . . . sorrow."

The folk in the verger's lodge noticed a little brown bird flitting about the Cathedral precincts, and admired its beautiful singing. "But it is a pity," said they, "that all that warbling should be lost and wasted far out of hearing up on the parapet." They were poor, but they understood the principles of political economy. So they caught the bird and put it in a little wicker cage outside the lodge door.

That night the little songster was missing from its accustomed haunt, and the Dark Image knew more than ever the bitterness of loneliness. Perhaps his little friend had been killed by a prowling cat or hurt by a stone. Perhaps . . . perhaps he had flown elsewhere. But when morning came there floated up to him, through the noise and bustle of the Cathedral world, a faint heart-aching message from the prisoner in the wicker cage far below. And every day, at high noon, when the fat pigeons were stupefied into silence after their midday meal and the sparrows were washing themselves in the street-puddles, the song of the little bird came up to the parapets—a song of hunger and longing and hopelessness, a cry that could never be answered. The pigeons remarked, between mealtimes, that the figure leaned forward more than ever out of the perpendicular.

One day no song came up from the little wicker cage. It was the coldest day of the winter, and the pigeons and sparrows on the Cathedral roof looked anxiously on all sides for the scraps of food which they were dependent on in hard weather.

"Have the lodge-folk thrown out anything on to the dust-heap?" inquired one pigeon of another which was peering over the edge of the north parapet.

"Only a little dead bird," was the answer.

There was a crackling sound in the night on the Cathedral roof and a noise as of falling masonry. The belfry jackdaw said the frost was affecting the fabric, and as he had experienced many frosts it must have been so. In the morning it was seen that the Figure of the Lost Soul had toppled from its cornice and lay now in a broken mass on the dustheap outside the verger's lodge.

"It is just as well," cooed the fat pigeons, after they had peered at the matter for some minutes; "now we shall have a nice angel put up there. Certainly they will put an angel there."

"After joy . . . sorrow," rang out the great bell.

THE PURPLE OF
THE BALKAN KINGS

LUITPOLD WOLKENSTEIN, financier and diplomat on a small, obtrusive, self-important scale, sat in his favoured café in the world-wise Habsburg capital, confronted with the Neue Freie Presse and the cup of cream-topped coffee and attendant glass of water that a sleek-headed piccolo had just brought him. For years longer than a dog's lifetime sleek-headed piccolos had placed the Neue Freie Presse and a cup of cream-topped coffee on his table; for years he had sat at the same spot, under the dust-coated, stuffed eagle, that had once been a living, soaring bird on the Styrian mountains, and was now made monstrous and symbolical with a second head grafted on to its neck and a gilt crown planted on either dusty skull. Today Luitpold Wolkenstein read no more than the first article in his paper, but read it again and again.

"The Turkish fortress of Kirk Kilisseh has fallen . . . The Serbs, it is officially announced, have taken Kumanovo . . . The fortress of Kirk Kilisseh lost, Kumanovo taken by the Serbs, these are tiding for Constantinople resembling something out of Shakspeare's tragedies of the kings . . . The neighbourhood of Adrianople and the Eastern region, where the great battle is now in progress, will not reveal merely the future of Turkey, but also what position and what influence the Balkan States are to have in the world."

For years longer than a dog's lifetime Luitpold Wolkenstein had disposed of the pretensions and strivings of the Balkan States over the cup of cream-topped coffee that sleek-headed piccolos had brought him. Never travelling further eastward than the horse-fair at Temesvar, never inviting personal risk in an encounter with anything more potentially desperate than a hare or partridge, he had constituted himself the critical appraiser and arbiter of the military and national prowess of the small countries that fringed the Dual Monarchy on its Danube border. And his judgment had been one of unsparing contempt for small-scale efforts, of unquestioning respect for the big battalions and full purses.

Over the whole scene of the Balkan territories and their troubled histories had loomed the commanding magic of the words "the Great Powers"— even more imposing in their Teutonic rendering, "Die Grossmachte."

Worshipping power and force and money-mastery as an elderly nerve-ridden woman might worship youthful physical energy, the comfortable, plump-bodied café-oracle had jested and gibed at the ambitions of the Balkan kinglets and their peoples, had unloosed against them that battery of strange lip-sounds that a Viennese employs almost as an auxiliary language to express the thoughts when his thoughts are not complimentary. British travellers had visited the Balkan lands and reported high things of the Bulgarians and their future, Russian officers had taken peeps at their army and confessed "this is a thing to be reckoned with, and it is not we who have created it, they have done it by themselves." But over his cups of coffee and his hour-long games of dominoes the oracle had laughed and wagged his head and distilled the worldly wisdom of his castle. The Grossmachte had not succeeded in stifling the roll of the war-drum, that was true; the big battalions of the Ottoman Empire would have to do some talking, and then the big purses and big threatenings of the Powers would speak and the last word would be with them. In imagination Luitpold heard the onward tramp of the red-fezzed bayonet bearers echoing through the Balkan passes, saw the little sheepskin-clad mannikins driven back to their villages, saw the augustly chiding spokesman of the Powers dictating, adjusting, restoring, settling things once again in their allotted places, sweeping up the dust of conflict, and now his ears had to listen to the war-drum rolling in quite another direction, had to listen to the tramp of battalions that were bigger and bolder and better skilled in war-craft than he had deemed possible in that quarter; his eyes had to read in the columns of his accustomed newspaper a warning to the Grossmachte that they had something new to learn, something new to reckon with, much that was time-honoured to relinquish. "The Great Powers will have not little difficulty in persuading the Balkan States of the inviolability of the principle that Europe cannot permit any fresh partition of territory in the East without her approval. Even now, while the campaign is still undecided, there are rumours of a project of fiscal unity, extending over the entire Balkan lands, and further of a constitutional union in imitation of the German Empire. That is perhaps only a political straw blown by the storm, but it is not possible to dismiss the reflection that the Balkan States leagued together command a military strength with which the Great Powers will have to reckon . . . The people who have poured out their blood on the battlefields and sacrificed the available armed men of an entire generation in order to encompass a union with their kinsfolk will not remain any longer in an attitude of dependence on the Great Powers or on Russia, but will go their own ways . . . The blood that has been poured forth today gives for the first time a genuine tone to the purple of the Balkan Kings. The Great Powers cannot overlook the fact that a people that has tasted victory will not let itself be driven back again within its former limits. Turkey has lost today not only Kirk Kilisseh and Kumanovo, but Macedonia also."

Luitpold Wolkenstein drank his coffee, but the flavour had somehow gone out of it. His world, his pompous, imposing, dictating world, had suddenly rolled up into narrower dimensions. The big purses and the big threats had been pushed unceremoniously on one side; a force that he could not fathom, could not comprehend, had made itself rudely felt. The august Caesars of Mammon and armament had looked down frowningly on the combat, and those about to die had not saluted, had no intention of saluting. A lesson was being imposed on unwilling learners, a lesson of respect for certain fundamental principles, and it was not the small struggling States who were being taught the lesson.

Luitpold Wolkenstein did not wait for the quorum of domino players to arrive. They would all have read the article in the Freie Presse. And there are moments when an oracle finds its greatest salvation in withdrawing itself from the area of human questioning.

THE CUPBOARD
OF THE YESTERDAYS

"WAR IS a cruelly destructive thing," said the Wanderer, dropping his newspaper to the floor and staring reflectively into space.

"Ah, yes, indeed," said the Merchant, responding readily to what seemed like a safe platitude; "when one thinks of the loss of life and limb, the desolated homesteads, the ruined—"

"I wasn't thinking of anything of the sort," said the Wanderer; "I was thinking of the tendency that modern war has to destroy and banish the very elements of picturesqueness and excitement that are its chief excuse and charm. It is like a fire that flares up brilliantly for a while and then leaves everything blacker and bleaker than before. After every important war in South-East Europe in recent times there has been a shrinking of the area of chronically disturbed territory, a stiffening of the area of chronically disturbed territory, a stiffening of frontier lines, an intrusion of civilised monotony. And imagine what may happen at the conclusion of this war if the Turk should really be driven out of Europe."

"Well, it would be a gain to the cause of good government, I suppose," said the Merchant.

"But have you counted the loss?" said the other. "The Balkans have long been the last surviving shred of happy hunting-ground for the adventurous, a playground for passions that are fast becoming atrophied for want of exercise. In old bygone days we had the wars in the Low Countries always at our doors, as it were; there was no need to go far afield into malaria-stricken wilds if one wanted a life of boot and saddle and licence to kill and be killed. Those who wished to see life had a decent opportunity for seeing death at the same time."

"It is scarcely right to talk of killing and bloodshed in that way," said the Merchant reprovingly; "one must remember that all men are brothers."

"One must also remember that a large percentage of them are younger brothers; instead of going into bankruptcy, which is the usual tendency of the younger brother nowadays, they gave their families a fair chance of going into mourning. Every bullet finds a billet, according to a rather optimistic proverb, and you must admit that nowadays it is becoming increasingly difficult to find billets for a lot of young gentlemen who would have adorned, and probably thoroughly enjoyed, one of the old-time happy-go-lucky wars. But that is not exactly the burden of my complaint. The Balkan lands are especially interesting to us in these rapidly-moving days because they afford us the last remaining glimpse of a vanishing period of European history. When I was a child one of the earliest events of the outside world that forced itself coherently under my notice was a war in the Balkans; I remember a sunburnt, soldierly man putting little pin-flags in a war-map, red flags for the Turkish forces and yellow flags for the Russians. It seemed a magical region, with its mountain passes and frozen rivers and grim battlefields, its drifting snows, and prowling wolves; there was a great stretch of water that bore the sinister but engaging name of the Black Sea—nothing that I ever learned before or after in a geography lesson made the same impression on me as that strange-named inland sea, and I don't think its magic has ever faded out of my imagination. And there was a battle called Plevna that went on and on with varying fortunes for what seemed like a great part of a lifetime; I remember the day of wrath and mourning when the little red flag had to be taken away from Plevna—like other maturer judges, I was backing the wrong horse, at any rate the losing horse. And now today we are putting little pin-flags again into maps of the Balkan region, and the passions are being turned loose once more in their playground."

"The war will be localised," said the Merchant vaguely; "at least every one hopes so."

"It couldn't wish for a better locality," said the Wanderer; "there is a charm about those countries that you find nowhere else in Europe, the charm of uncertainty and landslide, and the little dramatic happenings that make all the difference between the ordinary and the desirable."

"Life is held very cheap in those parts," said the Merchant.

"To a certain extent, yes," said the Wanderer. "I remember a man at

Sofia who used to teach me Bulgarian in a rather inefficient manner, interspersed with a lot of quite wearisome gossip. I never knew what his personal history was, but that was only because I didn't listen; he told it to me many times. After I left Bulgaria he used to send me Sofia newspapers from time to time. I felt that he would be rather tiresome if I ever went there again. And then I heard afterwards that some men came in one day from Heaven knows where, just as things do happen in the Balkans, and murdered him in the open street, and went away as quietly as they had come. You will not understand it, but to me there was something rather piquant in the idea of such a thing happening to such a man; after his dullness and his long-winded small-talk it seemed a sort of brilliant esprit d'esalier on his part to meet with an end of such ruthlessly planned and executed violence."

The Merchant shook his head; the piquancy of the incident was not within striking distance of his comprehension.

"I should have been shocked at hearing such a thing about any one I had known," he said.

"The present war," continued his companion, without stopping to discuss two hopelessly divergent points of view, "may be the beginning of the end of much that has hitherto survived the resistless creeping-in of civilisation. If the Balkan lands are to be finally parcelled out between the competing Christian Kingdoms and the haphazard rule of the Turk banished to beyond the Sea of Marmora, the old order, or disorder if you like, will have received its death-blow. Something of its spirit will linger perhaps for a while in the old charmed regions where it bore sway; the Greek villagers will doubtless be restless and turbulent and unhappy where the Bulgars rule, and the Bulgars will certainly be restless and turbulent and unhappy under Greek administration, and the rival flocks of the Exarchate and Patriarchate will make themselves intensely disagreeable to one another wherever the opportunity offers; the habits of a lifetime, of several lifetimes, are not laid aside all at once. And the Albanians, of course, we shall have with us still, a troubled Moslem pool left by the receding wave of Islam in Europe. But the old atmosphere will have changed, the glamour will have gone; the dust of formality and bureaucratic neatness will slowly settle down over the time-honoured land-marks; the Sanjak of Novi Bazar, the Muersteg Agreement, the Komitadje bands, the Vilayet of Adrianople, all those familiar outland-ish names and things and places, that we have known so long as part and parcel of the Balkan Question, will have passed away into the cupboard of yesterdays, as completely as the Hansa League and the wars of the Guises.

"They were the heritage that history handed down to us, spoiled and diminished no doubt, in comparison with yet earlier days that we never knew, but still something to thrill and enliven one little corner of our Continent, something to help us to conjure up in our imagination the days when the Turk was thundering at the gates of Vienna. And what shall we have to hand down to our children? Think of what their news from the Balkans will be in the course of another ten or fifteen years. So-cialist Congress at Uskub, election riot at Monastir, great dock strike at Salonika, visit of the Y.M.C.A. to Varna. Varna—on the coast of that en-chanted sea! They will drive out to some suburb to tea, and write home about it as the Bexhill of the East.

"War is a wickedly destructive thing."

"Still, you must admit—" began the Merchant. But the Wanderer was not in the mood to admit anything. He rose impatiently and walked to where the tape-machine was busy with the news from Adrianople.

FOR THE DURATION
OF THE WAR

THE REV. WILFRID GASPILTON, in one of those clerical migrations inconsequent-seeming to the lay mind, had removed from the moderately fashionable parish of St. Luke's, Kensingate, to the immoderately rural parish of St. Chuddocks, somewhere in Yondershire. There were doubtless substantial advantages connected with the move, but there were certainly some very obvious drawbacks. Neither the migratory clergyman nor his wife were able to adapt themselves naturally and comfortably to the conditions of country life. Beryl, Mrs. Gaspilton, had always looked indulgently on the country as a place where people of irreproachable income and hospitable instincts cultivated tennis-lawns and rose-gardens and Jacobean pleasaunces, wherein selected gatherings of interested weekend guests might disport themselves. Mrs. Gaspilton considered herself as distinctly an interesting personality, and from a limited standpoint she was doubtless right. She had indolent dark eyes and a comfortable chin, which belied the slightly plaintive inflection which she threw into her voice at suitable intervals. She was tolerably well satisfied with the smaller advantages of life, but she regretted that Fate had not seen its way to reserve for her some of the ampler successes for which she felt herself well qualified. She would have liked to be the centre of a literary, slightly political salon, where discerning satellites might have recognised the breadth of her outlook on human affairs and the undoubted smallness of her feet. As it was, Destiny had chosen for her that she should be the wife of a rector, and had now further decreed that a country rectory should be the background to her existence. She rapidly made up her mind that her surroundings did not call for exploration; Noah had predicted the Flood, but no one expected him to swim about in it. Digging in a wet garden or trudging through muddy lanes were exertions which she did not propose to undertake. As long as the garden produced asparagus and carnations at pleasingly frequent intervals Mrs. Gaspilton was content to approve of its expense and otherwise ignore its existence. She would fold herself up, so to speak, in an elegant, indolent little world of her own, enjoying the minor recreations of being gently rude to the doctor's wife and continuing the leisurely production of her one literary effort, *The Forbidden Horsepond*, a translation of Baptiste Leopoy's L'Abreuvoir interdit. It was a labour which had already been so long drawn-out that it seemed probable that Baptiste Lepoy would drop out of vogue before her translation of his temporarily famous novel was finished. However, the languid prosecution of the work had invested Mrs. Gaspilton with a certain literary dignity, even in Kensingate circles, and would place her on a pinnacle in St. Chuddocks, where hardly any one read French, and assuredly no one had heard of L'Abreuvoir interdit.

The Rector's wife might be content to turn her back complacently on the country; it was the Rector's tragedy that the country turned its back on him. With the best intention in the world and the immortal example of Gilbert White before him, the Rev. Wilfrid found himself as bored and ill at ease in his new surroundings as Charles II would have been at a modern Wesleyan Conference. The birds that hopped across his lawn hopped across it as though it were their lawn, and not his, and gave him plainly to understand that in their eyes he was infinitely less interesting than a garden worm or the rectory cat. The hedgeside and meadow flowers were equally uninspiring; the lesser celandine seemed particularly unworthy of the attention that English poets had bestowed on it, and the Rector knew that he would be utterly miserable if left alone for a quarter of an hour in its company. With the human inhabitants of his parish he was no better off; to know them was merely to know their ailments, and the ailments were almost invariably rheumatism. Some, of course, had other bodily infirmities, but they always had rheumatism as well. The Rector had not yet grasped the fact that in rural cottage life not to have rheumatism is as glaring an omission as not to have been presented at Court would be in more ambitious circles. And with all this death of local interest there was Beryl shutting herself off with her ridiculous labours on *The Forbidden Horsepond*.

"I don't see why you should suppose that any one wants to read

Baptiste Lepoy in English," the Reverend Wilfrid remarked to his wife
one morning, finding her surrounded with her usual elegant litter of dic-
tionaries, fountain pens, and scribbling paper; "hardly any one bothers
to read him now in France."

"My dear," said Beryl, with an intonation of gentle weariness, "haven't
two or three leading London publishers told me they wondered no one
had ever translated L'Abreuvoir interdit, and begged me—"

"Publishers always clamour for the books that no one has ever written, and turn a cold shoulder on them as soon as they're written. If St.
Paul were living now they would pester him to write an Epistle to the
Esquimaux, but no London publisher would dream of reading his Epistle to the Ephesians."

"Is there any asparagus in the garden?" asked Beryl; "because I've
told cook—"

"Not anywhere in the garden," snapped the Rector, "but there's no
doubt plenty in the asparagus-bed, which is the usual place for it."

And he walked away into the region of fruit trees and vegetable beds
to exchange irritation for boredom. It was there, among the gooseberry
bushes and beneath the medlar trees, that the temptation to the perpetra-
tion of a great literary fraud came to him.

Some weeks later the *Bi-Monthly Review* gave to the world, under the
guarantee of the Rev. Wilfrid Gaspilton, some fragments of Persian
verse, alleged to have been unearthed and translated by a nephew who
was at present campaigning somewhere in the Tigris valley. The Rev.
Wilfrid possessed a host of nephews, and it was of course, quite possible
that one or more of them might be in military employ in Mesopotamia,
though no one could call to mind any particular nephew who could
have been suspected of being a Persian scholar.

The verses were attributed to one Ghurab, a hunter, or, according to
other accounts, warden of the royal fishponds, who lived, in some unspecified century, in the neighbourhood of Karmanshah. They breathed
a spirit of comfortable, even-tempered satire and philosophy, disclosing
a mockery that did not trouble to be bitter, a joy in life that was not pas-
sionate to the verge of being troublesome.

"*A Mouse that prayed for Allah's aid*
    Blasphemed when no such aid befell:
A Cat, who feasted on that mouse,
    Thought Allah managed vastly well.
Pray not for aid to One who made
    A set of never-changing Laws,
But in your need remember well
    He gave you speed, or guile—or claws.
Some laud a life of mild content:
    Content may fall, as well as Pride.
The Frog who hugged his lowly Ditch
    Was much disgruntled when it dried.
'You are not on the Road to Hell,'
    You tell me with fanatic glee:
Vain boaster, what shall that avail
    If Hell is on the road to thee?
A Poet praised the Evening Star,
    Another praised the Parrot's hue:
A Merchant praised his merchandise,
    And he, at least, praised what he knew."

It was this verse which gave the critics and commentators some clue as to the probable date of the composition; the parrot, they reminded the public, was in high vogue as a type of elegance in the days of Hafiz of Shiraz; in the quatrains of Omar it makes no appearance.

The next verse, it was pointed out, would apply to the political conditions of the present day as strikingly as to the region and era for which it was written—

"*A Sultan dreamed day-long of Peace,*
    The while his Rivals' armies grew:
They changed his Day-dreams into sleep—
    The Peace, methinks, he never knew."

Woman appeared little, and wine not at all in the verse of the hunter-poet, but there was at least one contribution to the love-philosophy of the East—

> *"O Moon-faced Charmer, and Star-drowned Eyes,*
> *And cheeks of soft delight, exhaling musk,*
> *They tell me that thy charm will fade; ah well,*
> *The Rose itself grows hue-less in the Dusk."*

Finally, there was a recognition of the Inevitable, a chill breath blowing across the poet's comfortable estimate of life—

> *"There is a sadness in each Dawn,*
> *A sadness that you cannot rede:*
> *The joyous Day brings in its train*
> *The Feast, the Loved One, and the Steed.*
> *Ah, there shall come a Dawn at last*
> *That brings no life-stir to your ken,*
> *A long, cold Dawn without a Day,*
> *And ye shall rede its sadness then."*

The verses of Ghurab came on the public at a moment when a comfortable, slightly quizzical philosophy was certain to be welcome, and their reception was enthusiastic. Elderly colonels, who had outlived the love of truth, wrote to the papers to say that they had been familiar with the works of Ghurab in Afghanistan, and Aden, and other suitable localities a quarter of a century ago. A Ghurab-of-Karmanshah Club sprang into existence, the members of which alluded to each other as Brother Ghurabians on the slightest provocation. And to the flood of inquiries, criticisms, and requests for information, which naturally poured in on the discoverer, or rather the discloser, of this long-hidden poet, the Rev. Wilfrid made one effectual reply: Military considerations forbade any disclosures which might throw unnecessary light on his nephew's movements.

After the war the Rector's position will be one of unthinkable embarrassment, but for the moment, at any rate, he has driven *The Forbidden Horsepond* out of the field.